Sunrays on the Beachhead of the New Creation

Sunrays on the Beachhead
of the New Creation

A Novel

JOSHUA E. LIVINGSTON

Illustrated by Judy Langemo Roth

WIPF & STOCK · Eugene, Oregon

SUNRAYS ON THE BEACHHEAD OF THE NEW CREATION
A Novel

Wipf & Stock
An Imprint of Wipf and Stock Publishers
199 W. 8th Ave., Suite 3
Eugene, OR 97401

www.wipfandstock.com

PAPERBACK ISBN: 978-1-5326-1640-2
HARDCOVER ISBN: 978-1-4982-4017-8
EBOOK ISBN: 978-1-4982-4016-1

03/24/21

For Bethany Anne

The liberating dawn of the new creation is death?
God's idea of good news includes the crucifixion of
God's son, of the world, and of human beings?

—J. Louis Martyn

Contents

Contents

Permissions

Except where noted, all biblical references from the New Revised Standard Version Bible, copyright 1989, Division of Christian Education of the National Council of the Churches of Christ in the United States of America. Used by permission. All rights reserved.

Scripture quotation marked (NIV) are taken from the Holy Bible, New International Version®, NIV®. Copyright © 1973, 1978, 1984, 2011 by Biblica, Inc.® Used by permission of Zondervan. All rights reserved worldwide. www.zondervan.com The "NIV" and "New International Version" are trademarks registered in the United States Patent and Trademark Office by Biblica, Inc.®

Scripture quotation marked (AV) from The Authorized (King James) Version. Rights in the Authorized Version in the United Kingdom are vested in the Crown. Reproduced by permission of the Crown's patentee, Cambridge University Press.

Quote from J. Louis Martyn taken from his essay, "The Apocalyptic Gospel in Galatians." *Interpretation: A Journal of Bible and Theology*. Volume: 54 issue: 3, page(s): 246–266. Issue published: July 1, 2000.

Illustration for *Ideas and Beliefs* based on a photo by Shadman Ahmed.

Werner Herzog's "Minnesota Declaration" delivered at the Walker Art Center, Minneapolis, Minnesota April 30, 1999. The six-point addendum was conceived as a response to the Walker's request for Herzog to reconsider his manifesto in light of Trump-era "alternative facts" and "fake news." https://walkerart.org/magazine/werner-herzog-minnesota-declaration-2017-addendum

Acknowledgments

This work was started in 2008 in St. Petersburg, FL, and was finished in 2020 in Indianapolis, IN, with a significant onset of writer's block in Chattanooga, TN in between.

I remember with fondness all the folks that have had a hand in shaping this work, whether they were aware of it or not. It all began with encouragement from my wife, Bethany, who has remained with me as I would (more often than not) inwardly process our life experiences through writing. Thank you, love. This work is dedicated to you.

Thank you to the group from Englewood that met to read early drafts together and provide feedback: Cheryl Klette, Wil Peoples, Claire Price, Diana Marine, and Joe Bowling. I also want to mention the many short, but significant, conversations in the car with Jim Aldrich.

I am particularly grateful to Sophia Muston for her keen copyediting abilities, feedback, and ongoing encouragement throughout the revision process. Grace and peace, Soph.

Finally, a heartfelt debt of gratitude to Judy Roth, who helped conceived the initial draft of this work over a decade ago. Your work has continued to inspire me over and over again as the text continued to develop a life of its own. This whole project is really my endeavor to find the words to somehow match the aesthetic integrity of your imagery.

J.E.L.
November 19, 2020
Indianapolis, IN

Prologue: Daybreak

My dearest,
Please take a moment to step outside.
Look above you. I will do the same.
What do you see? I see clouds.
They are huge, white and puffy and
I'm tempted to want to just fall
into them. But please don't focus
on the clouds, for they are constantly
changing, always moving, and what's
more, they're not really there like
you think they are. No, my dear,
look past the clouds and see the same
sun that I am looking at, even now.
Let it warm you. That is the same
It never changes. It will continue
to let it warm me, too, and it
is this warmth that brings us
together.
                    Love, Mother

Christ Event Horizon

The Earth weathers two worlds. There is a way that seems right to man that leads to death. There is a death that seems to lead man towards the right way.

Life in the cloud is a transitory vapor, an everyday dance between the storms of life and a sunny disposition. It's how the world tourniquets. Our own work of healing. Dressing our gashes. Blessing our feelings. Our goodness clouds judgement. Of the Father of Lies, the events of this world will break us, for better or worse.

The blue sky is cracked like a cosmic wound, wisdom gushing forth like light. It's how we see what we see. It's how we know what we know. It's grotesque, it's splintery, it's invasive. It's the dawn of a reality hewn of a cross. If we are wise, the event of Christ will shake us, for better or worse.

What she's saying is, to live into one is to die to the other.

I still carry around her tattered letter, with its terrestrial cautions. She still speaks. Each day needs new clouds dispersed. Sometimes I'm blind in the choking fog. Other times are sublime, fit for prayer and poetry. Still others are overcast, but a truth remains: Cast adrift in an ultraviolet ocean, the sprays immerse us in the mist and waves cascade upon us with a tidal force, yet we scarcely perceive it. If we're not careful, we'll cook.

I go in search of empty worlds awaiting radiation. The sojourn of a wounded warrior, the trespasses of a happy little failure, en route through events to a sudden, hidden end. But between you, me, and the warmth of the sun, what good's an omniscient narrator who's diminished to know nothing but Christ, and him crucified? Good for nothing, I suppose, and for everything else.

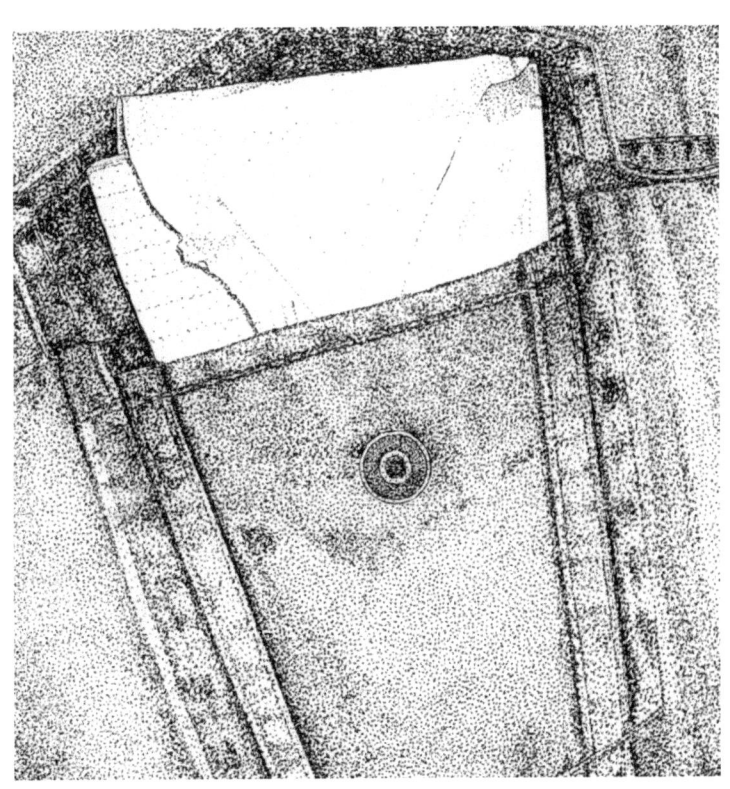

Encounters

The new creation is no specter. Nor is it a respecter, of lands, cities, boundaries, or epochs. It is for all places in all times. Being no place in particular, it is that much harder to perceive. Like a thief in broad daylight, if he's worth his weight in theft, he won't be thieving when you can see. He looks like you and me. In fact, he is you and me. Really, it's less about the people and the place than it is about the eyes and the ears.

If the new creation were to fall in a forest, but there were no witnesses, would it proclaim the good news?

What good is a journey to discover that which you already possess? The kingdom of God is like a man with a missing limb stumbling upon a cardboard box. Limping up to it, he peers inside only to find a folded up and bloody leg.

Come, Lord Jesus. Sever me.

The Silent Spark

This is for the different. As far as journeys go, there isn't much distance to cover. You'll see what sort of good a map is. Perhaps you can look up from your book even now. Who's in the room with you? Tune your ear to the silent spark. The new creation is an odorless gas leak. Religion is the smell of sulfur used to detect and stop it.

Holy Water

We were a bit confused when we passed by her casket and saw that Grandma was still smiling. The dead don't show their teeth. Everyone kept saying she lived a good life. They say she lived a full and complete life.

What is a good life? And how does anyone know when a life is complete?

I know that there was more that could have been done. There was always more we could've done. There was more that could have been done thirty years ago.

Nobody says that the purpose of life is to see who can live the longest.

Why is it now a cliché to question suffering?

Somewhere along the way we began to think of good as a modifier. A way to describe no suffering. Grandma called good a noun, said it was a thing held in common. The good needed to be modified, not the other way around. It needed to be modified by others. Moving from a noun to a modifier makes moral assumptions about others' corroboration of a thing's goodness and beyond that, we're not even sure we're talking about the same things. I'm good. I'm a good. I'm a good that needs no modifying. Because I am, therefore good.

Looking at Grandma's memorial candles, I test my logic. Is fire good? I suppose we can symbolize whatever spirituality or spiritualize whatever symbolism. Or I can just flick this one candle over and let the flame take over this entire altar. Would that fire be good? No, the question is: Is fire *a* good? The answer: Sure, but how, and for whom?

What about water? Is this water good? Jesus, it's holy water. It's now dawned on me that I am doing everything I can to avoid the pain of mourning.

They always say, "life is good." Well, for some. But for most, that's a lie. But if we ask is a life *a* good, then we're onto something. Of course it's a good and how we handle this question determines everything, I suppose. Is life its *own* good? What sort of good is life? And for whom? How is life different from any other good? Or, is it a good that somehow transcends modification? Do we really need to qualify life? Do we need to fight for life at all costs? Did we fight for Grandma's life at all costs? The answer to that last one is no. We can't afford all costs.

I love her. But I love the feeling of not having to deal with her loss more than I love her. Otherwise, I'd accept her death. I would have accepted her death years ago. I would accept my death.

I'm terrified that if I allow myself to accept that the good of life is not life itself but something else, then I'm accepting death. Why does that seem morally wrong? Grandma is still preaching the good news. I suspect it has less to do with death than the contraction "I'm." Yeah, we all use it. We use it because we really believe we are more efficient than God.

99 *Faithful Sheep*

There was once a shepherd who had a hundred sheep to care for. But there was one who would always drift off by herself and inevitably, the shepherd would have to leave the ninety-nine others to fetch her. This became so routine that the ninety-nine were trained to wait together until the shepherd returned.

So it began as a typical day—the wayward sheep had gone missing and the shepherd took his leave. Usually, it only took a few hours to retrieve her, but this day seemed a bit different. Sheep are not very smart, but even they realized something was amiss. They don't know much, but they do know their shepherd.

The daylight hours began to dwindle: three o'clock, six o'clock, nine. Eventually it became dark and some of the sheep began to grumble amongst themselves.

"He's left us."

"Perhaps he's had enough."

"It's all her fault."

"Why can't she just stay put?"

But some of the others would have none of this poisonous gossip. "When has our Master ever been unfaithful to us? He said he would return. And you all know very well that he would not stand even one second of this slanderous talk! Tear doubt out of your hearts! Let us be watchful, for his coming is near!"

Well, the hours turned into days. The sheep were steadfast and they remained together in their waiting. But that's not to say that there was never any complaining or some degree of impatience. Of course there was—they're only sheep.

By the third day, all murmuring had ceased. Some were even on the verge of mourning. They had all stopped chewing their cud.

Their thoughts and prayers were fully exhausted. There was nothing left to hold on to. But only in this stillness could the voice of their Master finally be heard.

"Come, little lambs!"

It was a hoarse and faint cry, but once the ninety-nine realized what they were hearing, they all turned their ears in expectant unison. Again:

"Come, my dear ones!"

The voice was from the depths of a nearby cliff. The sheep all shook their wooly heads and thought, "All this time we felt so alone and he was actually so near!"

The flock inched nearer to the cliff and peered over the edge. The sight below shocked them and they all gasped. The wanderer had fallen into the rocky chasm. The shepherd had made a courageous attempt to save her, but in doing so, he lost his footing and fell. There he lay, bloodied and bruised, holding the limp body of his dear deserter.

The shepherd's eyes were shut tight and his calls to his flock were not commands. They were simply cries of the heart. He had no idea he was even speaking out loud. So even though the sheep had answered the call, he continued to cry out:

"Come, little ones!"

The ninety-nine looked at each other with a fiery glow in their eyes. Not knowing where the path would lead, they simply obeyed. One by one they each stepped over the edge of the cliff to a rocky death below. Lo and behold, they were where they always wanted to be: right at the side of their Master.

A Modern Samuel

Samuel's dad sent the boy off to count sheep because he wanted to see if that actually worked. He knew that it probably wouldn't, but it could buy him some time. Parents, you get it. You love your children to death. But if they don't go to bed at some point, you might stop loving your children.

Samuel obediently went back to bed, although on his back. Do people who lie on their backs really intend to go to sleep? This is the position best suited for counting imaginary animals. Samuel never met a sheep that didn't bore him, so he chose scorpions instead. One, two. . .

"*Samuel!*" A voice struck that resembled a father. He followed it down the hall, only to be sent packing. His dad wasn't known for emotional availability.

Back in bed, rather than simply scorpions inching along in a line, he counted scorpions lifting their tails up over their bodies, stinging various animals. One—*sheep*. Two—*deer*. . .

"*Samuel!*" The interruption was definitely audible. Trepidating down the hall, light on his feet, he peeked around the corner. Yeah, his dad definitely wasn't calling him.

This time, he turned on his side with the covers pulled up tight under his chin.

"*Samuel!*"

The boy screamed in terror down the hall.

"What the hell, Sammy?"

Through panicked breath, "Dad, I think God's calling me."

Samuel's dad put those thoughts to rest.

"Son, this crazy world wants you to think you're something special. Do you know that? And do you know why this world wants you to think that? It's because they want you to buy as much as you can so that you believe you are special. It starts with toys, then it's clothes, then it's cars, then it's education, then it's a job. . . Son, it never ends. And especially with Christians, they'll hang it all on God. God wants you to be special. God's gonna call you. He's gonna call you to have that toy, those clothes, this car, go to school here, work this job. . . I'm not jerkin' ya' son! The religious folk really believe this!

"Now I don't doubt that you're hearing voices. I don't even doubt that God's callin' you. But listen, don't get caught up in mixing those up. God's callin' all a' us. I just want you to know what callin' means. You gotta get this, because it's really funny. It's really a cosmic joke. And it's a damn good one, son. Yes, we're called by God, but really, we're like the last picked in gym class.

"Am I right? Think freckles. Think curly red hair and a belly hanging out below a too-tight green Adidas tank top. Matchin' shorts and socks. I think God picks some a' us only cause we know we're not really gonna amount to a hill a' beans and we won't be steppin' on anybody tryin' to. Listen, if you didn't know Jesus from Sunday School, you couldn't tell him from any other hangin' criminal. He was somethin' special. Son, you're not special. I'm not special. But just remember: God's not callin' for anything special. He's just not interested in cowards."

Samuel swallowed an invisible pit. You know where it went.

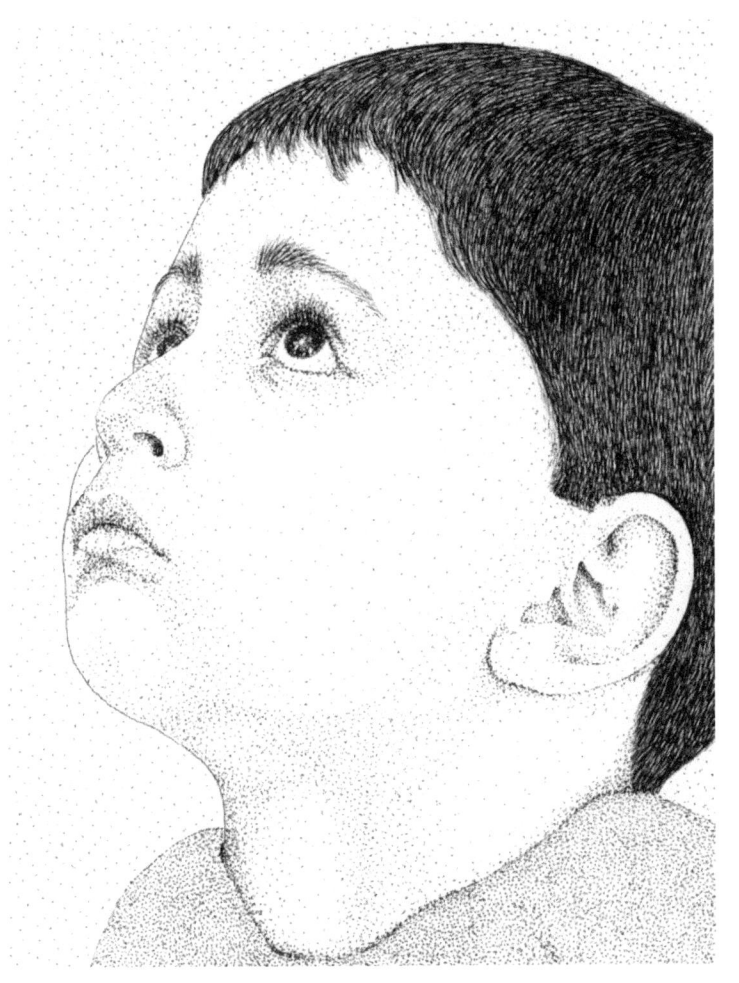

The Sad Shepherd

Another shepherd slunk along the pathway with his head hung low. His sheep were scattered and now his dog had gone off.

"What is wrong with my sheep?" he wondered to himself. "Day after day for many a year have I taken these sheep from pasture to pasture and countryside to countryside and now this—they've abandoned me. They have truly lost the way and I can only pray for their salvation."

The sad shepherd was so deep in thought and his eyes turned so downward that he almost ran into someone that was standing right in front of him. The shepherd attempted to walk around the mysterious stranger, but for some strange reason, he could not push past him. Maybe he was awed by the way this man stood with such authority; how it seemed he stood upon a firm foundation, as if he was rooted there. The shepherd, however, felt just the opposite. It was as if the ground was opening up underneath his feet and he was just hanging there, about to drop into a black abyss.

But he continued to hang on. "May I pass by here, sir?" the sad shepherd stammered.

The moment became even stranger when the stranger responded, "The good shepherd lays down his life for the sheep. The dog runs away because a dog does not care for the sheep. The good shepherd knows his own and they know him."

The shepherd's heart sunk. It felt as if it had dropped through his feet and into the hole above which the rest of his body somehow still hung.

The stranger turned his back and began to walk away.

"Wait!" the shepherd called out somewhat sheepishly. He lowered his head, closed his eyes, and set his jaw. "Tell me, stranger. What good is a shepherd, anyway?"

When he picked his head up and opened his eyes, he found that the stranger was gone. There was nothing more to be said to a shepherd more concerned about shepherding than about sheep.

The Role of Bears

*From there Elisha went up to Bethel. As he
was walking along the road, some boys came
out of the town and jeered at him. "Get out
of here, baldy!" they said. "Get out of here,
baldy!" He turned around, looked at them
and called down a curse on them in the name
of the Lord. Then two bears came out of the
woods and mauled forty-two of the boys.*

-2 KINGS 2:23–24 (NIV)

I've never met a prophet I didn't like. I think that's a relief. Because
if you're on the wrong side of a prophet, well, that's it.

I don't know how they do it. I'm not sure they do either. Any
fool can say they have God on their side. But when a prophet says
it, you can be sure he's full of it.

Instead, I tend to look for things like fire and dying.

Some of us get hung up on, "Is there a God?" What's a question like, "Is there a God?" to a prophet? There's any number of
things a prophet will get hung up on as an answer to that question.

When your friends start throwing rocks at a prophet, begin to
rethink what you mean by friend.

And lastly—and I found out this one the hard way—if your
certainties provoke you to attack an innocent man who claims to
be a prophet and God sends out bears in his defense, begin to rethink your certainties, the role of bears, and the question, "Is there
a God?"

Interlude: At Sea

*(A brief aside, with fragments of
thought on Matthew 14:22–33)*

*Immediately he made the disciples get into the boat and go on ahead
to the other side, while he dismissed the crowds. And after he had dismissed the crowds, he went up the mountain by himself to pray. When
evening came, he was there alone, but by this time the boat, battered
by the waves, was far from the land, for the wind was against them.*

The scene is set in almost contemporary fashion. Jesus seems
so distant, and in more ways than one, he is. He is in the presence
of his Father. Meanwhile, as the light is chased away by darkness,
his followers find themselves exiled at sea, with nothing but one
another.

*And early in the morning he came walking toward them on the
sea.*

Note the passage of time. There is a darkness, unspoken. But
alas, the Savior draws near and the sun also rises. He comes, and in
a manner most confounding, even impossible.

*But when the disciples saw him walking on the sea, they were
terrified, saying, "It is a ghost!" And they cried out in fear. But immediately Jesus spoke to them and said, "Take heart, it is I; do not be
afraid."*

And so the dialogue begins. Let us begin with sensational-
ism. What can stir us into the greatest frenzy? What immediate, if
irrational, conclusions can we draw? What can we do to distance
ourselves from a terrifying reality? Again, very contemporary

questions. Yet, Jesus, against all common wisdom, chooses to engage this confusion, and penetrates to the core of the matter.

Peter answered him, "Lord, if it is you, command me to come to you on the water."

Ultimatums. The art of the deal.

He said, "Come."

I'll see you. And raise you.

So Peter got out of the boat, started walking on the water, and came toward Jesus. But when he noticed the strong wind, he became frightened, and beginning to sink, he cried out, "Lord, save me!"

The act of faith or the grave mistake? Peter strikes out on his own. We often talk about the step toward Jesus, not even seeing the step away from his people.

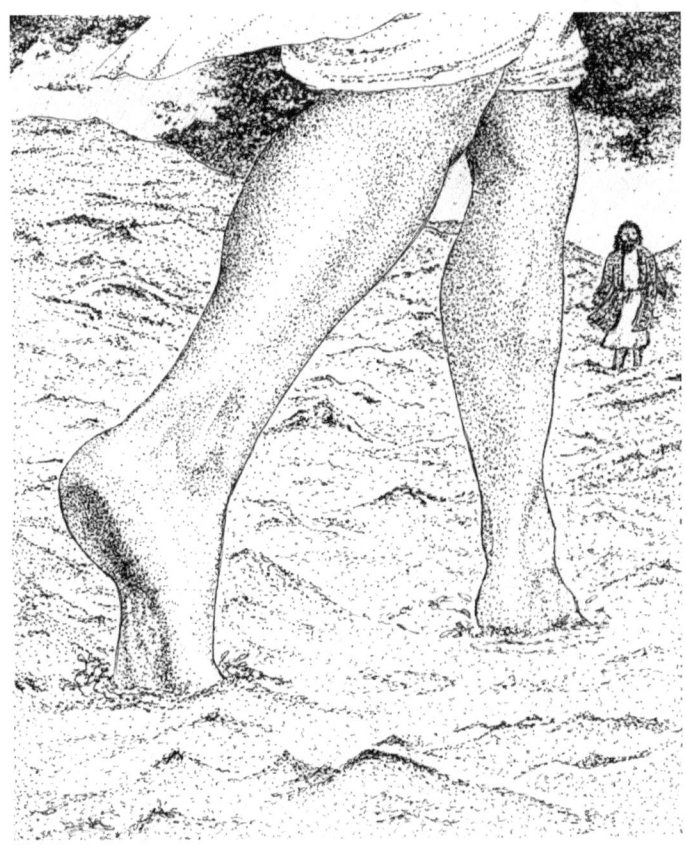

Jesus immediately reached out his hand and caught him, saying to him, "You of little faith, why did you doubt?"

Why is this story instructive? To valorize the virtues of extraordinary acts and heroic deeds? To frame the story of faith between "me and Jesus?" Does doubt here signify the weakness of underperforming?

When they got into the boat, the wind ceased.

Perhaps the doubt was in the boat: the integrity of the boat (read: Ark) and its inhabitants. Perhaps Jesus' invitation to "Come" was not intended to test the faith of Peter, but simply the direct response to Peter's negotiation: "Lord, if it is you. . ." Rather than follow Jesus alone, together, we invite Jesus aboard.

And those in the boat worshiped him, saying, "Truly you are the Son of God."

Dolphin Blues

"*What do children know* about politics?" he says. "Nothin," he says, looking for a friendly debate over an oversized plate of food he probably shouldn't be eating.

"I don't know," I said. "Politics is about agency, right?"

I could tell I was starting to go over his head.

"In what ways do children contribute to society? Typically, we think of citizenship in terms of agency."

I may have lost him. It's so obvious when someone stops listening.

"Yet for children, agency can consist of political presence, rather than simply political action." I have this thing where I just keep talking, even when no one's listening. It's not 'cause I like to hear myself talk. It's 'cause I seriously doubt my own intuitions about whether someone is actually listening. I am wrong about most things more often than not.

"Their agency may or may not be passive, but it can certainly be passed over. The very presence of children changes the tenor and timbre of a room, and the quality of this change—attentiveness, humility, curiosity, concern, wonderment, directness—these are the elements of what could be described as a virtuous society."

"You got a point there, buckaroo."

See, he was listening.

"My dad used to take me fishin," he said. "And he would just make up these little word pictures, or parables, I don't know what you'd call them."

"Oh, yeah?" I try to promote active listening. Not 'cause I want to make sure people know that I hear them, but 'cause I seriously doubt I will actually listen well if I don't. But more often than not, I'm thinking about my gestures of active listening.

"School was out. The bell rang and hundreds of these little baby mullet were on the loose."

He'd already started. I didn't realize he had begun recounting a story his dad made up about how daylight savings time can bring on an existential crisis for sea life.

"Typically at this time it was still light out, but more recently, it has been quite dark at dismissal and many of the fishlets wondered to themselves, "Why has the great light above gone out? What is the meaning of this darkness? Their teacher, a cantankerous old puffer fish who was exhausted from chasing after unruly fingerlings all day, was on his way home and did not want to be bothered.

"'Teacher, teacher! What can you tell us about the great light above? Where has it gone?'"

"In an effort to make the annoying little fish go away, he simply retorted, 'School is out. My job is done. Go home to your moms and dads!'

"Good one, right? Well, obviously not satisfied with that answer, the fish decide to swim down to the bottom and ask the old crab. He was a very learned professor, full of knowledge, but the youngsters didn't know that with such intelligence often comes cynicism.

"He says, 'Children, I've never seen a great light such as you speak of. I've heard others speak of it, and many have even described its wonders, but for this old crab, the seafloor is what I know and there is no light here at all.'

"Well, the mullet kids had seen a great light. They were sure it existed. But where had it gone? Confusion reigned as they began to posit theories and bicker amongst themselves. Then, as they began to ascend back to the surface, suddenly a net dropped down out of nowhere.

"Uh-oh," I interjected. Again, active listening.

Without missing a beat, he continues. "Then, a great sonar blast grabbed all of their attentions. A mother dolphin crossed their path, redirecting the young school a bit farther back underwater.

"Relieved that they were all safe, and grateful for the mother's wisdom, they were all in agreement as to whom to ask next. 'Mother, where has the great light gone? And what is the meaning of this darkness?' And you know what Mother Dolphin said?"

I waited, assuming he would just tell me. But he didn't. He just stared at me with this ridiculous smile on his face.

"No, I have no idea what Mother Dolphin said."

"She says, 'Life is like a can of tuna. . . You never know what you're gonna get!"

And with that he cracked himself silly, belting out an obnoxious falsetto guffaw and an ensuing cough.

"Get it? 'Cause they kill dolphins and call it tuna?"

"Ah, yes." I attempt to appease him. "I get it."

Afternoon Beachhead

Behold, the end! The children look below as waves of lava encroach from all sides. The Earth has met her fiery fate and now this lofted landing is the only territory left declared "safe."

Anchored staunchly, the children share the hope of a new civilization. A common vision is their only hope. The face of each child, in turn, represents the abiding diversity and boundless ingenuity afforded them. How can they not survive?

Each member of this new society scouts the occupied land. Some prefer the high road, establishing a strategic vantage point. Others keep a low profile, content to shape a foundation, address critical internal demands. Somewhere in the middle, organizers build bridges between established enclaves and take stock of each contribution for the good of the cause.

One child decides he will be responsible for food. He gathers fruit, prepares, stores, saves seeds, and packages sustenance for distribution.

Another ensures each sector meets safety standards. She inspects every child's area, instructs them on habitation procedures, and draws up a system for zoning and use. Some areas are for personal use, some areas are shared, and some are off-limits for safety reasons.

Education: what personal experiences and abilities does each member of this community bring, and more critically, how are these transferred? A child pledges to create a map of assets and cross-reference them with the various tasks required for the building up of the new world.

A fourth listens, observes, and documents this story of survival as it unfolds. Many ask: Is this an essential function of a new nation? A people without a story are a people without a future. It is determined: without the storyteller, the people cease to be a people at all.

Shouldn't the new nation have a flag of identification? Yes, a badge of honor, survival, and commitment. It would be the banner of hope under which each one would pledge their very lives.

On and on, each child contributes according to the breadth of their ability and the strength of their imagination. A society of amateurs, experts are not applicable. Over time, what develops is an ecosystem of gathering, storytelling, discovery, and play. A children's courtroom, organized by branch, a haven for balancing, reasoning, dreaming, discerning.

And so, the adventure rolls on, beyond sunset, into the dusk of curfew.

A child is called home. A critical loss, and an occasion to celebrate the gift and contribution of a fellow soldier!

We gather to tell more stories. What has been accomplished? How will we continue tomorrow? A loss of this magnitude creates a monument in time. It is an act of sacred remembrance. Eventually, we are all called home. Yet, our place continues to tell our story.

Evol Island

Greetings, weary traveler. We are Legion and welcome to our sacred island, an angel hair's breadth off the gulf coast of Florida. After centuries upon centuries of wandering, penetrating, and pillaging, we've settled here, as a community among communities, with honor among thieves, sharing a harbor with the likes of snowbirds, spring breakers, pirates, and tycoons. You may be more familiar with our beloved ancestors, the cursed herd of Gadarene, the ancient sounder from whom we share a direct lineage.

With our neighbors, we've pioneered an outlaw commonwealth, rooted in a theology of vacation. That is to say, our only hope is in escape. This foundational truth has been passed down to us from generation to generation through the sacred history of our foreswine. Our way of life is built on the only virtue we know, as it was demonstrated on that fateful day, and imitated faithfully by our mothers and fathers: total annihilation. You've heard of man's golden rule. Ours is the pink of flesh: the way of salvation is through death.

We have heard the story recounted to us, time and time again, of the man who is the founder and creator of our world. It is to him we owe all. Our forefather, shunned by a society upheld by the underpinnings of purity—a laughable pretense if there ever was one—this man was shamed, rejected, and pitied, cast off to fester with the bones, carcasses, and rotting flesh of those who had perished. Chained like a rabid beast, they say he was possessed, but we proclaim his ecstasy. He truly was the living among the dead.

We are familiar with his torture. We empathize with his misery. We embody his rage. And to this very day, we are persecuted, but not forsaken, struck down, but not destroyed. Like our father, we stand face to face with the one they call the Son of God. We know him as the Tormentor, our chief Enemy, damning and invasive. And somehow, he knows us and has infiltrated our way of annihilation. Our only hope is to flee.

Legend has it, as the curses of our forefather were passed to the herd of our foreswine, the man prophesied: From the Son who's flee'd, is freed indeed. Our father was transfigured, and it was our descendants who sank into the mud of madness and depravity for him, sacrificing themselves unto a watery grave.

And so now we live, as a testament to the grain of the universe that we feed upon daily. On this godforsaken island, we feast upon death together as a sign of the possession we await for the entire world.

Bikini State

August 9, 2012. Tampa Bay, Florida.

Ghosts drifted over the pockmarked pavement. Spirits lingered, resurrected by a brief summer rain. When seeking any signs of life, the absence of presence can be palpable.

Martin and Marcus were quite familiar with the old joke about the Chevy Nova. And now they're living punchlines, dripping down the shoulder in the sweltering heat with their thumbs erect but leaning.

About a half a mile was all that Martin would commit to. He wasn't afraid to travel long by foot. No, he was more pessimistic about relying on the hands of others when he had two that were perfectly capable at his disposal.

Marcus, meanwhile, relished the opportunity for discovery. Landscapes of the unknown, the yonder and the stranger. Yes, he was pessimistic about his ability to do anything mechanical, but he had every faith in the abundant capacity acquired wherever two or more are gathered.

So after taking about twenty-five hundred steps, Martin turned back. It was a fork in an otherwise linear thoroughfare. Marcus pulled out his phone, tapping every resource that artificial intelligence could possibly actualize.

Even though Martin was returning to the source of their problem, it felt like a homecoming. He rolled up his sleeves, and while the handle on the passenger door was hot to the touch, it didn't deter him. It opened with a comfortably recognizable creak. He sat down, popped open the glove box and rummaged through years of unused insurance policies looking for anything that he could actually get his hands on.

Marcus, pale blue in the face, like a canvas being stretched for the sun to lay on splotches of reddish rash, was beginning to panic. While his life was a virtual success by our society's every standard, it was situations like these that seemed to remind him that his life skills were just that—virtual. He always teased Martin because Martin would refuse to buy car insurance through him, but now he was overcome by the realization that insurance cannot start your car.

Martin pulled out an awl from the glove box. He actually laughed out loud, because he knew that Marcus didn't even know what an awl is, let alone how to use it or why it's in his glove box in the first place. He threw it back in and got out of the car. Discerning Marcus's professional strengths, and thereby his habits and priorities, Martin slipped under the car. It was immediately evident the oil filter had not been changed for some time. The story was coming together for him when his phone rang.

Marcus rattled off all of the reasons why Google says cars overheat. It was a frantic attempt to demonstrate some last-ditch remnant of self-worth, an effort to elude the question he knew was coming from the other end of the line.

"Marcus, when's the last time you changed your oil?"

After a silent ride in a wrecker, and with the Nova towed back to Marcus's house, Martin grabbed a plastic tub and went to work. All Marcus could do was pray, or rather, question whether God cares about cars. He concluded God probably did have thoughts about our technological society.

Martin popped up from under the car and curiously began rummaging in the glove box. He pulled out the awl and asked, "Marcus, do you have a hammer?"

Marcus took a full seven minutes to locate a hammer, but he did have one. He handed it to Martin, intentionally averting his eyes from Martin's alpha male gaze.

As Martin's legs protruded out from under the car, Marcus observed his boots, brand non-descript, and jeans, broken unbeknownst. To Marcus, his style spoke of sheer apathy and utter self-confidence. Looking down at his own form-fitting chinos and scuff-free chukkas, he contorted uncomfortably in his own self-consciousness.

Bangs and clangs commenced as Martin was driving the awl through the base of the oil filter canister and hammering on it to shock the filter loose. He may as well have been piercing and turning loose Marcus's stuck-tight ego. The fact that his twin brother has to work on his classic '68 Chevy Nova for him because he doesn't actually know how to maintain it has reduced to him to a puddle of self-induced psychoanalysis.

For all the ways the web-based life claims connectedness, those very connections presuppose gaps, distance, emptiness, and estrangement. This is the essence of virtual reality.

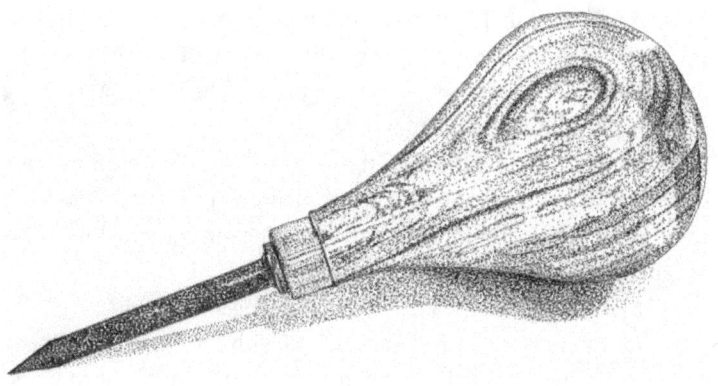

Black Widow Blowback

It was a dreary day when an army of black widow spiders descended upon the colony of working-class Ant Hill. The black widows, in their greed, decided they wanted to produce three times as many webs as they had previously been able to make. So they captured the insects of Ant Hill and put them to hard labor, teaching them the art of web-spinning.

The ants had many different reactions to this corporate take-over. Many of them grumbled to themselves, longing for life back on the colony. They would do their work halfheartedly, reluctantly, and spitefully.

Others took pride in their new found ability to spin silk. The black widows rewarded the most prideful ants. The ants that made the most beautiful webs were put in charge of enforcing the hard labor of their fellow ants.

There were also ants that set out to convince the black widows of the error of their ways. They would tell them that life was not all about how well you could spin a silky web or how powerful you could become by lording over others. They had many, many words and would sometimes speak for hours on end. But the spiders figured out how to shut them up. They would simply put them in charge of other ants, just like they did with the prideful ants. Then all the talking would stop and things would go on just as they were before.

But there was one final group of ants that demonstrated an entirely new way—a protest ant's work ethic, you could say. It was the way they had always worked—each ant would carry up to five thousand times their own weight for the good of the whole colony. These ants banded together and carried their responsibilities in the same way they had at Ant Hill, only now their work was for the good of the black widow webs. Instead of each ant producing its own web, like the spiders had taught them, these ants would all work on a web together, singing, whistling, and cracking jokes. This way confused and hardened the black widows even more. Hard labor was not supposed to create harmony, merriment and joy.

It was around this time that hard working ants began to disappear. There is a deep-seated understanding among ants that at any given time one may get stepped on. Their life together was necessarily founded and sustained in courage. The more ants wound up missing, the harder they would work. They simply could not be killed off. The more that each ant leaned in to what it means to be an ant, the more strengthened and unified they became. As it turned out, the Ant Hill colony was not taken over. It was alive and well in the webs of the black widows.

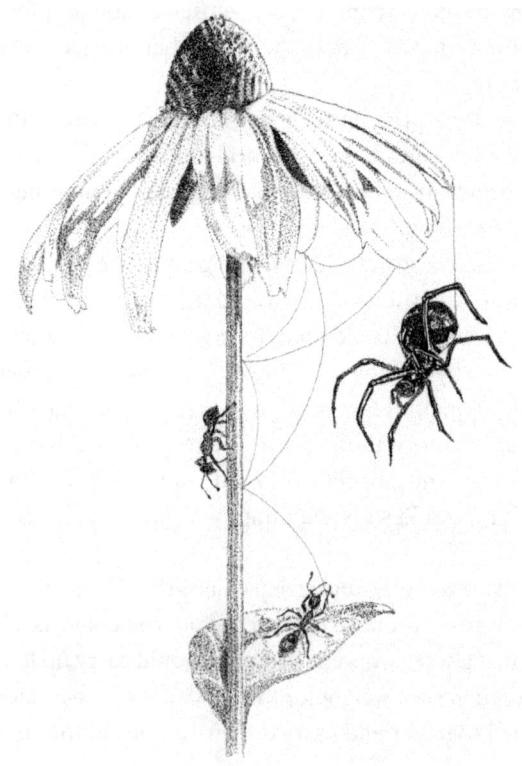

Lessons from Babel

A wise man once said, "The world reveals itself to those who travel on foot." Exit Babel, where at once we were struck with a blindness of rationality. With the tongue reduced to a mere flap of flesh, even less than ornamental, there was nothing left to accomplish but to walk away and start anew.

After the first fifty miles of straight sojourn, your body reminds you that you're meant to belong somewhere. At five hundred miles, your mind is no longer along for the ride. Your eyes roll around in your skull and the landscape begins to bleed. Light, color, and form are still present, but no longer attached to signs and symbols, or rather, they become empty. Indeed, language is God's loophole.

Then it occurred: With the tower subdued, its memory a wake of delirium and disorientation, all at once, a vision. And I could not tell if I was dreaming or awake. Brick upon brick, for I had handled so many, their coarseness remaining forever on my fingers, I was somehow still home, and building. Even now, five hundred miles away, we continue to build that tower. The tower was building us, or so we hoped. But no, this was not a tower. This time, with each step, I could hear my breath from inside my ear. Each breath was a brick pulled from the oven. Each step inserted it into a wall. The farther I went, the taller it stretched, course by course. Until I stopped. And there I stood, face to face with a wall so tall it divided the Earth. Wide, gray, and monstrous, it cast a shadow so large it was as if the sun only rose on one side. And every one of us imagines we are on the side of light.

When everything is illuminated, there isn't a need for questions. When all that exists are answers, life becomes an endless choice. At a crossroad with infinite directions, all the world is made of signs. To make it anywhere in life, you'd better learn to read. The joke is, there are no destinations. There is no point of Origin. There is no point. Only empty signs.

Necessarily, the Other. In a world of shadow, all one has is trust. Subject to mercy, there are no leaders. Everyone's a leader. Rather, every subject is also a predicate. The only way to move is through another. In a life like this, there is no "I." Rather, we each become a sign. Only signs of everyone else.

I continued to walk along the wall, fingertips tracing the bricks like Braille. A nagging certainty shadowed me. Bereft of belonging, there was only longing. With all these answers in life, I have to find the right question. So, I began to scale the wall. Onlookers observed, faces displayed dismay, and horror was heard in gasps of breaths and clicks of the tongue. I do not know who these people are, or if they really exist.

I imagine nobody on the side of light ever heard from me again, and each endeavor to erase me from their memories. But this strange fever dream persists. I no longer know who's dreaming. Beams of new Light break through the wall from the side of shadow, a Light so luminous that the old light seemed like darkness.

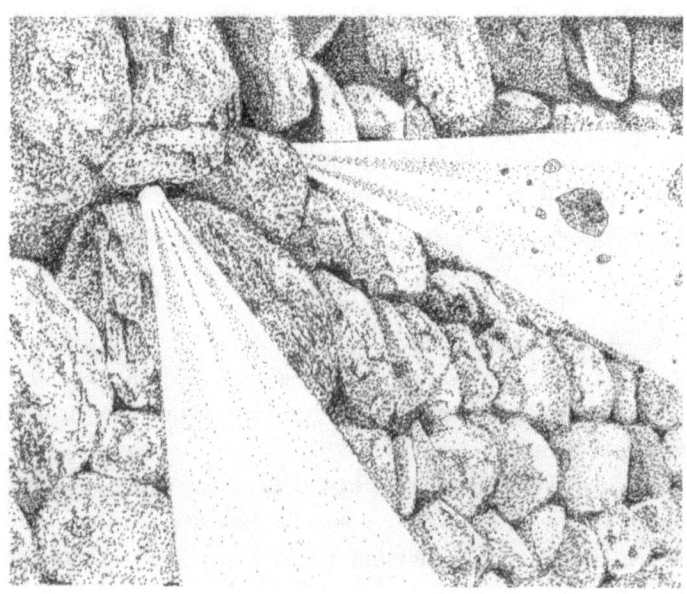

Lessons from Babel

When I arrived, I awoke. Of course, arrival means nothing as I belong nowhere. I am not the one to make an interpretation, but from this vantage point, there are many lessons to be learned. Even God knows, when the people are as one, there is nothing that can befall them. Yet to what end is the gift of our oneness given? Today, I have seen the tragedy of the double illusion. A community constituted, by necessity, cannot exist but by over and against. Whether it's God or nation. Fragmentation follows, but God can redeem a broken, scattered people, while nation cannot. Anyway, what good is a wall? A sign to nowhere on a ground shared by all.

The Breach

October 1, 1990. Mt. Bethel, Pennsylvania.

Overcast gray on an unusually crisp autumn, edging on early afternoon. This sleepy farm town is still in mid-morning meditation. It must be Saturday. Meanwhile, the Survivor Club is in session. Every young'un, with an attitude ten to fifteen years older than their actual age, agree to meet. Cameron provides the straws. Cut up in two-inch sections, each takes one between their fingers, puffs, and exhales a cloud of cooled carbon dioxide.

I recall the warped boards culled from the garages of our fathers. I remember the stern glares signifying the maturity of make-believe business. There were maybe twelve of us. Each kneeling in turn, inspecting the splintered shards, the rusty nails, bent and exposed. Someone had breached our sacred space. We were victims of village vandalism, where everyone knew everyone, so this wasn't so much a case of whodunit, as much as what-to-do-about-it-now.

Mario had slick, black, wavy hair frequently flipped back and tucked behind his ear. His pursed lips could emit a salacious smirk: shallow mischief below a shadow mustache. With only a few inches on most of us, his aura still loomed large. Maybe five years our elder, he was the envy of each of us, yet also intimidating enough for us to avoid him. A true teenager, exploring the limits of newfound liberty, Mario exercised his free will to flex his self-appointed authority over the entirety of our fledgling enterprise.

We were upended. And when the foundations shook, our sense of security succumbed. With our shelter in shambles, our circle searched for understanding, questions unending. Tim was

one grade above, but two years our elder. A de-facto leader when our courage was curtailed, always able to relay the basics.

I see him standing tall, slender like the trees which balance our beams. The memory is silent, but I see him speak with his hands, a benign coercion, like a preacher or a politician. We, the circle, sit with legs crossed and necks crooked, under his spell.

His message contained prodigious sophistication, the work of a youthful elder statesmen, although never appointed, as our approach to politics was as personal as it was anarchistic. The club had established a culture of charisms, which, as we now understood, ended up with each competing until one assertively authorizes himself. That someone was Mario.

The crossroad consisted of this: The Survivor Club continues status quo, as if it could, given this corruption of corporate security, or we constitute a community that moves us from mere survival to flourishing. Can we come together to find a common commitment? To fund a common good? Are we a club for us or a club for all?

I remember resisting the urge to avenge our fort. Pushing back a passion all too pleasing. Yet, for the first time I felt the peace of freedom, not from my ability to act on my own behalf, but by voluntarily obliging myself to a structure of fractal belonging. My good was their good was Tim's good was Aaron's good was Kevin's good was Christian's good was Cameron's good was Mario's good. . .

It was confrontation or conciliation. We could either take the club to Mario or we could invite him into our Club. But this time it wouldn't be about survival. In the end, we could not call ourselves a club at all. Rather than simply rebuild a fort, we moved beyond the form, to fortify a vessel we called Kinship.

Dark Abbey

The monks of Dark Abbey first gathered hundreds of years ago during a time in which the entire world was engaged in raging warfare. Nobody on earth cared for each other and everybody was always fighting about something, so this poor band of merry men decided that they would take leave of it all and start a brotherhood founded in peace and justice in the wilderness.

This community was planted at least three days walk from the nearest village and the monks liked it that way. The monks built many little houses using nothing but clay brick and then surrounded themselves with very tall walls of mud and stones. These walls were so tall that it took longer for the sun to rise there than at any other place on Earth. So, they named the place Dark Abbey. By the time it was all said and done, they had essentially founded their own village in the middle of the desert. It was a mighty conglomerate of simple homes, a township unto itself.

No more would they hear the clang of swordplay, the groans of the wounded, or the outbursts of anger and hatred. But neither would the villagers see peace and justice demonstrated for them.

Well, many years went by and the first brothers who started the community passed on and unfortunately, so did their vision of peace, justice, and brotherhood. This new generation of monks was raised in total isolation from the world, but the world was very much within them. There was constant bickering and arguing and a steady stream of gossip and slander.

One brother liked to cook meat and potatoes. Another preferred a strict diet of vegetable and fruit. One brother liked to sing hymns to God. Another found solace in sacred chant. One brother would sit in his study all day in prayer and holy reading. Another would be plowing the fields or sawing lumber. Nobody could agree on what was best for the Abbey as a whole.

Then one day it happened that all the wars of the surrounding nations came to a grinding halt. The long-awaited Messiah had returned to the war-torn Earth to ultimately establish his everlasting reign of peace; all nations surrendered and bowed before him on their knees. However, since the old monastery was entirely cloistered off from the affairs of the world, it was many years until the news of this peaceable kingdom finally reached the Dark Abbey. Yet when it finally did, the brothers became fearful of their lives being disrupted. They began to dig large underground tunnels in which to dwell. There they spent the rest of their lives under the Earth and were never heard from again.

And so it goes: living in a state of perpetual darkness will eventually lead to blindness. The eyes lose their ability to possess light, by which all things are made known.

Interlude: 33 AD

(A written response to my friend who told the dolphin tale. I think we're on the same page.)

Jesus tells his disciples that unless they change and become like children, they can never enter his kingdom. Oftentimes, we can characterize children by their purity, simplicity, or innocence. We tend to want to distinguish a romanticized "childlikeness" from a more realistic "childishness." But perhaps Jesus doesn't welcome children because of any unspoiled, inherent virtues they might possess, but because they demonstrate for us a constant need for a shepherding authority.

Autonomous self-governing adults are allergic to authority. A society constituted by atomized individuals is inherently alien to a common good, and averse to a common life. But the social location of the child is that of a dependent. Children do not possess agency apart from an authority.

What happens in a room full of children left to their own devices? Complete chaos. If there is not an authority in place to shepherd and guide the unbridled freedoms of children, little ones get hurt. So it is with the so-called "mature." Our society shapes us into citizens characterized by those same unbridled freedoms. We call it liberty and we fight for our rights.

A boy quietly pinches his little brother. The little brother cries out loud. The parent is busy cooking dinner in the other room. The older brother whispers threats to quiet his brother. The younger brother retaliates in fear. The older brother asserts his dominance. The parent is overwhelmed so avoids the situation.

Crying and shouting ensues. Followed by biting and pulling of hair. The parent erupts. . .

We can imagine there was a reason the disciples wanted children to stay away. Their very presence requires that we must attend to them. Which disallows us from simply attending to ourselves. Yet Jesus says, "Let the little children come to me. . ."

In Matthew 18, when Jesus outlined a skeletal narrative for reconciliation among his disciples, he was not recommending a recipe for interpersonal conflict resolution. Rather, he was instituting and identifying his authoritative presence in the form of his body, the church. If one brother offends another, it is not simply a matter of two brothers, but a matter of the entire body, of which each member is authorized to engage the situation, for the good of the whole.

The common good of people cannot be maintained by autonomous individuals left to their own judgement. With complete freedom of choice, the state of being human is characterized by conflict. Therefore, for the Christian on this side of the kingdom, all authority is carried in the cross and characterized in the death of Christ, so that all may become children of God.

Under the Evening Sky

"Those are nice enough words and all."

I sincerely wondered if he actually read it.

"Listen here, I'ma head on down to the woods later. I got this spot."

The spots always meant places for drink, smoke, carbs, and arguments. The spots were always set for two.

"Well, you know, I've got some things," I said.

He wasn't biting. "Nah, it's not one of them spots. This is the spot to end all spots."

He had my attention, anyways. He had my attention, always.

"You know why I have a problem with authority?"

I shook my head. Active listening.

"You know why I question 'em? 'Cause this place is damn cold. This here world is in the shitter. And there ain't no one to turn to. I mean, no one. No government, no religion, no family. . ."

It so happens my friend is an orphan. Always wandered. Mostly alone. "But there is you and me." I attempted to bind us as one.

"This spot is me headin' out. You know the freighter that snakes through them woods? I'm punchin' my ticket out. Tonight."

He hadn't read it.

"Well, that's one way to handle the present evil age, I suppose."

"Ain't no handlin'," he said. "I can take up my arms or my fists or whatever and put up a good fight. But there ain't no haltin' the machine. The game is rigged. The jig is up. And I ain't a violent man. A man like me can only handle so much."

"What about God?" I asked. "What about a benevolent authority? What about the cross?"

"I believe he's *been* on there!" he said. "I believe he *lives* on that there train."

He's right about that. "You know, I believe you're right. There's no setting things right from this vantage point." I think we're on the same page. There's no ascending to blessedness for us mess.

My friend took his leave that night. Hopped aboard the tail end of a three-mile long freight train en route to anywhere but here. I stayed behind, in expectation of something else. We are on the same page. Only the train can't take him off the page and I know someone took a match to the page and the fire is headed this way.

Old Shadrach

A legend tells of an old man who lived alone in a hut at the tail end of his life. The hut resides on the outskirts of the city, where the forest becomes very thick. I've been told that it is still intact. This old man is revered by all the city dwellers because many claim he lived such a full life that others only dream of what he's experienced. Few would dare to venture out into the woods to meet him, for many have gone and not returned. Some say they got lost in the wooded maze. Others say the old man's hut is the entranceway to heaven.

Whatever the reason, one theory about the man resonated more than all the others, and it is this story that I will proceed to tell. This version of the man's life claims that he is actually Shadrach— friend of Meshach, Abednego, and the prophet Daniel. There is one incident in particular that made believers out of many in the city.

A band of five adventurous children from the city's slums decided to flee their poor surroundings in the middle of the night in order to find the gateway to heaven. Whatever danger may lie ahead, they thought, had to be better than the misery of the lives they were leading.

So the children cut up some small logs and made torches to light their path in the woods. For the entire journey, barely a word was spoken by any of them.

About six hours into the woods, they decided to stop. Their feet were very sore and the bugs had become almost unbearable. As they kept waving torches around their heads, they could hear the bodies of the bugs singeing in the flames.

As they sat around quietly, wondering if they had made a mistake, they heard the sound of a stick breaking in the dark woods behind them. Someone or something had stepped on it. All five of the children stood up, turned around, and peered into the darkness. The footsteps were surely getting closer and closer, when suddenly, as if out of nothingness, the old man appeared.

The children were scared stiff. Silence reigned. His very presence spoke to them about holiness and grace—things that these hardened few were hardly familiar with. They could never put it into words, but something Mighty and Wonderful was in their midst. And here was just a frail old man, hunched over, about four and a half feet tall. His hair was long and gray and he wore a tattered, tan-colored robe.

The man offered a slight smile, revealing rotten teeth.

The children all looked at each other. They stood upright, making every attempt to appear like they were good, prim, and proper young adults. After a few of some of the longest minutes that ever ticked away, one of them mustered the courage to speak.

"Sir, can you tell us about the gateway to heaven?" They were each shaking. "We've heard that, perhaps maybe, that you were the gatekeeper?"

The old man signaled for the children to gather around him. And so they did, in circle formation. Then, he finally spoke.

"Children! Hold your torches high!"

Slowly, and each in turn, the children lifted their flames overhead.

"Gently tilt them downward."

The flames and anxieties all remained raised. The old man demonstrated prophetic patience. His hunched frame poised, only his eyes made any movement. One by one, eventually, the torches began to tilt.

"Now, children. Turn your torches on yourselves!"

Incredulous, and on the edge of panic, thoughts moved around the circle like lava waves. They reasoned: could this be why none of the others had ever returned from the woods? Has this crazed old man brought them to their deaths? Despite the palpable presence of doubts, a mysterious fire was kindled that night—white hot and blazing bright. It beckoned the children to trust the old man. And so they dipped their torches upon their own heads like Whitsun tongues. Flames engulfed the entire circle of children, and would you believe, none of them were burned! Each one stared at the other in wonderment, hearts and eyes wide open. Then, when they looked back to the center of the circle, they saw not one man but two! The old man was on his knees before the Other—the one whom they knew was the Son of God.

May the fire come upon us all, if only that we may be met by the Presence.

A Modern Isaac

"Dad," he said, "I want to know Jesus."

"No you don't," I said.

We were walking up a hill.

"Sure, I do!" he said.

"What do you know about Jesus?" I queried.

"I know he's God, but he died, and he came back, and he forgives us so we can live forever."

Now I'm really intrigued. "Are you going to live forever?"

"I am now."

"How do you know that?"

"Because Jesus loves me!"

We stopped at the crest of the hill and I began scanning the area.

"What if I told you that you are going to die. Everyone dies."

"Of course, I know everyone dies, Dad. But God will bring us back, too. *Then* we live forever."

"Aaah, I think I get it." I began gathering large stones and branches. "But what if I told you that I really struggle with believing all that about Jesus?"

"I think I'd have to pray for your soul, Dad, because you don't believe."

"Maybe you should. But what if I told you I'm not sure it much matters whether I believe or not?" I averted my eyes, but I could feel his ultraviolet gaze. It was so warm. "Son, I'm not sure you need to worry about knowing Jesus quite yet. You may find he's not at all what you expect." I started to shake as I stacked the stones and wood.

"What do you mean? If he loves me, he'll always protect me, right?"

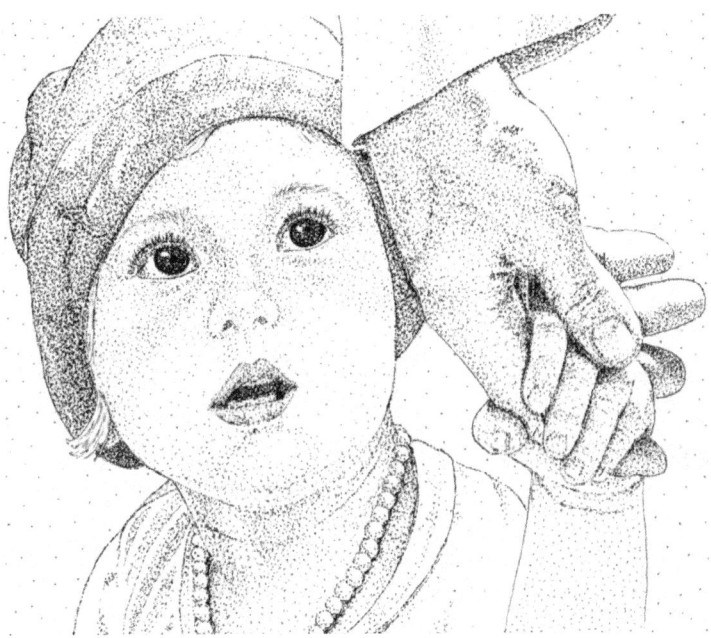

I stood up straight and exhaled deeply. "You know, son, I'm not so sure." I pulled out my knife.

"What are you doing, Dad?"

Suddenly, a ram emerged from a nearby thicket, startling us both.

"Oh, thank God," I thought to myself. "What a strange and terrible story I'm in."

World, Interrupted

"God help us," *was* the last blasphemy breathed. Clad in nondescript black, with a peeling leather backpack and baseball cap, shadow cast over his puke pale visage. Now, his very own esophagus seemed to slowly choke him.

Six months of internet research, fits, starts, mail-orders, wires, parts, and chemicals. The logical conclusion of this world's hopeless trajectory. A disruptive act of a God denied, not unlike the blue death of crisp, white polar landscapes at the hands of almighty humankind.

Wrapped his contraption with jaundiced newspaper he raided from his recycling bin. It was his gift to the world.

He cast out into the sea of isolated souls, unsuspecting of the alarm that was about to be apocalypsed unto them all. Some kid skipped by. No, he swallowed, the more purity present, the starker the contrast, the clearer the message. "Do this in remembrance of me."

A strict schedule. Three and a half minutes until the time was fulfilled. Standing upon a bench, he held up a fist high above his head, eyes closed, chin lowered. His first crime was blatant theft. Tommie Smith and John Carlos, from the 1968 Summer Olympic Games.

Words. What words? Many words raced through his mind. He needed the words that would match the ecstasy of his protest. And yet, stage fright, and fragments. I've been to the mountaintop. . . Blessed are the poor. . . Don't ask what your country. . . A mind full of clichéd soundbites was the second of the day's crimes. Aesthetic crime.

With his anxious effort to create a vibe with a silence, he lost the time. He pulled out his phone and felt the rush of pink into his cheeks. He swallowed hard, sending his heart downwards. More pink, more cheeks. The phone was on silent. And the timer read 00:00.

Our prophet's crimes never exceeded two for the day. He looked up, incredulous, and half-conscious. About twenty people had their own phones out, videos rolling, a meme in the making. The death of an ego on a park bench.

Demonstration Plot

A *deep breath of* blue autumn air, the texture of morning dew slides over every sleeping pore. The rustle of leaves draining green. Exhale, the spirit mist dissolves. Dawn graces the landscape, hues of peach with lavender tint. Cumulus clouds sop up the sun's orangeish sheen. A tender breeze envelops, drawing me nearer to my labor, nearer to the earth. I start with a spade shovel, the fog of midnight's memories still lingering fresh. The chickens tussle straw, dropping their beaks, plucking at signs of life that only they discern.

The shovel slides in without protest, a gummy communion of last week's straw and poultry droppings. As I lift a spadeful, a subtle suction, the earth is off to work, taking leave with a goodbye kiss.

Further afield, the unmistakable aroma of freshly cut grass, gleaming with silvery beads of late summer cold sweat. I glean all clippings from the previous evening's mow, gathering them into a dull gray pit, constructed with broken cinders and sealed with the past year's soil.

With a wheelbarrow chock-full of a steaming mass of waste and hay, I lift, roll, and stammer my way towards the cold, rectangular casket of earth's decaying matter. With a single heave, the moist marriage from the poultry pen eclipses the soft bed of grass blades.

Next is the pitchfork. A shallow stab and a twist. A turn over, tilt, release, and repeat. They've told me all about carbon and nitrogen, but I fail to discern the poetry in that. I suppose instead, I've learned to dance. I place my feet upon those of Mother Earth and let her guide me through the slow rhythms of the four seasons.

I take a step back to survey my workmanship. A field dedicated to death and decomposition. I had a dream of wandering through a cemetery, or at least it seemed that way. Only somehow, I knew the place was permeated with life. Rows of makeshift gray stones, along a blackened brown fence with many sagging pickets. Each depicts a season.

The empty wheelbarrow, always a relief to lift, leads me as I gently roll towards the last bin of blocks. A peer inside, another deep inhale. Coffee-colored, lush, and loamy, the soil pulsates, breathes, and teems with life, a microcosm household and habitat. A worm society and granular government.

Again I lift my spade, and with a tremor and a prayer, I penetrate the porous soil, carry and inspect this miraculous material, and ceremoniously spread it over the steel bed of the barrow. I repeat the rhythm like a rosary.

As the mysteries of morning are exposed to the openness of afternoon prosaics, I lean on my spade and observe with reverence the landscape of our organic garden. People often ask me, "What do you like to grow?" I always tell them that I only grow one thing: Soil.

Ideas and Beliefs

A young man approached his father.

"Father, I believe I should be feeding the poor."

The father replied, "That's a good idea!"

The next day, the young man approached again.

"Father, I believe I should care for the elderly. They are forgotten!"

His father replied, "That's a good idea!"

The day after that, a third time.

"Father, I believe that I should comfort the dying. How they suffer!"

Again, the father, "That's a good idea!"

Finally, the father called after the young man.

"Son, take your little sister to the park and teach her how to swing."

The young man replied, "But father, I believe that which I do unto the least of these. . ."

"That's a good belief," said the Father.

"But watch out for ideas and beliefs.

There's little else that can turn God away."

The Blue Session

An old blue truck remains parked beneath the city bridge. Isolated and idle, its sagging tires sit very depressed. There was a time when beneath the bridge cars and trucks would merrily roll about on their morning joy rides. Traffic patterns engraving the habits of membership, vehicles would take their time, the rules of the road playing out more like virtues than observance. Storefronts would line this street and their owners would stand posted with a broom and a smile. At the red light, you'd be sure to wave through the windshield. The stranger was scarce. But now it's quiet and still, except for the constant whoosh of the freeway overhead. And the blue truck sits alone.

I was lumbering along by myself beneath this bridge when I came upon the old blue truck. I stopped and gave it an inordinate amount of attention. The windshield was a two-way mirror, the truck, off, the beaten empath.

I decided to reroute my routine going forward. Day in and day out, I walked by this truck, detailing, but not in the way a vehicle would prefer. This was mere analysis. Cobwebs stretched between the side mirrors and the door. Rust had begun to eat away the paint, in some places leaving ominous, gaping holes.

During one particular session, I broke through. Shards from the passenger-side window scattered about, I took a hard look inside. The cab was flooded with memories. It maintained the scent of dignity, contribution, and agency. And there was a single key left in the ignition. Perhaps together, we could start again?

The Owl and the Dead Man

A night owl in the forest inquired, "Who? Who?"

The man looked behind himself and tossed the answer over his shoulder, "I am lord and master!"

The cool night pondered silently.

The night owl continued to interrogate, "Who? Who?"

The man crouched down, staring down the serpent. "I am keeper of this land!"

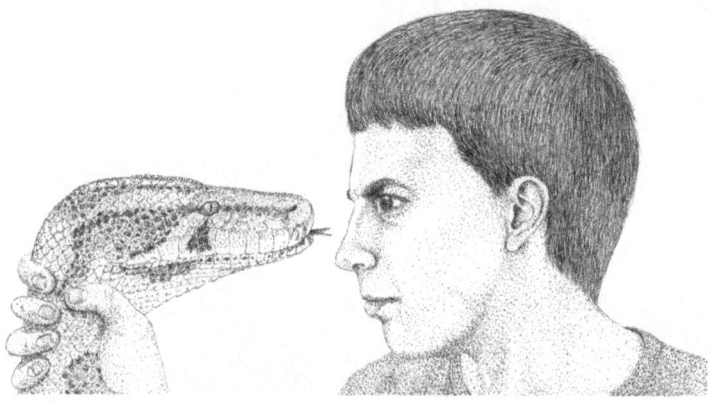

The rustling leaves laughed.

Again, the night owl asked "Who? Who?"

In retreat, the man proclaimed, "I am a friend! I come in peace!"

The darkness is his closest friend.

The night owl catechized, "Who? Who?"

The man lay prostrate with his face in the dirt. "I am a stranger! From where have I come and to where will I go?"

The wind chimed in, waxing wrath.

The night owl insisted, "Who! Who!"

The void converged upon this soul, by grace. "I am a dead man. To the dust I shall return."

Fireflies emerged to meet the moon, amidst a cloudland cascade.

The night owl rejoiced, "Amen and amen! May eternity blossom forth from this holy ground!"

The Light of Gold Mountain

The worst had happened. As the gold miners were heading towards the small beam of light at the far end of the cave, a mellow rumbling overhead slowly grew into a mighty roar. And just like that, the final ray of light was snuffed out.

It was pitch black. Not a single miner could see even an inch beyond his nose.

What were they to do? For the longest time, there was nothing but frustration: yelling, cussing, raging, and crying. Then there was despair: quiet, sobbing, weeping, and praying.

Hours went by and the miners said barely a word amongst themselves. Each was deep in thought—what did their lives amount to now? What good were they for the world? Would people miss them after they were gone? Would people even notice they were missing? Questions like these tormented each man for hours on end, which turned into days on end, which became weeks and weeks with no end in sight.

It came to pass one day that one of the men, John they called him, decided to take things into his own hands. He was going to fight for his life. He knew that they were basically buried alive, but how could they have forgotten? They were buried in a gold mine!

John saw this great misfortune as a once in a lifetime opportunity. However, he knew that he would have to convince others to work with him. They were going to beat this mineshaft. If they couldn't break their way out, they would rob it and pillage it until nary a cent was left to take.

"Riches!" John cried aloud. "Glorious, glorious riches! What more could we want?" he reasoned. Every day we came to this dirty mine so we could find gold. Now look at the bright side! We have everything we've ever longed for right here at our fingertips!"

Strange as it seemed, some of the men began to come around. Many had lost all hope. At least John offered some sort of purpose in the midst of all their pain. He was right. They were now rich. They were literally surrounded by—covered in—gold, gold, and nothing but gold! So off they went, every which way, to collect and stockpile their booty.

Other miners, however, didn't quite buy it. As John and his band of merry men went deeper and deeper back into the dark corridors, these other men tried to remember the last place they had seen the light. As dark as it was, these men could see beyond the cold, closed, confines of the cave. So, they came to agree on a particular direction and together they began digging through rock, shale, clay, mud, gold, diamond, whatever. It didn't matter. They had seen the light and that was what they were striving for.

Well, a few more weeks went by since John and his men had set off. All the leftover rations were long gone and the miners who remembered the light were just about ready to give up and collapse when—

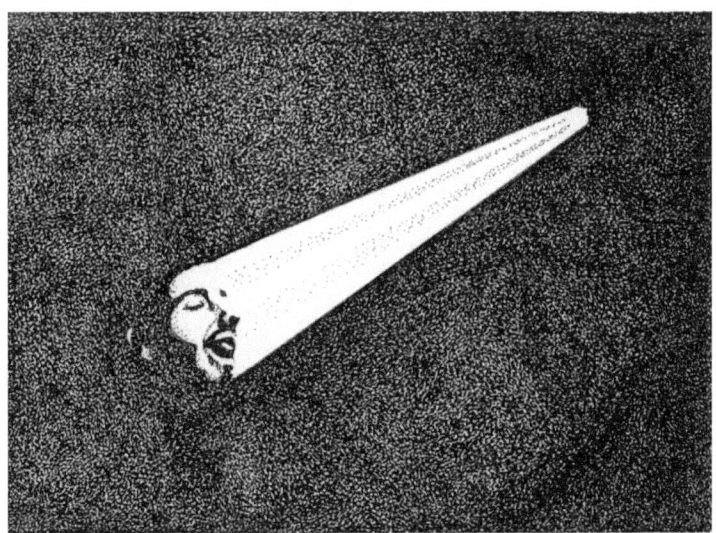

A tiny ray of light pierced the darkness like a laser and all the men fell to the ground temporarily blinded. Had they finally broken through? Had they found the long-lost light? No, years later they would say the Light had found them.

Once the miners had completely broken through, they decided to go back in and find the others. But just about all of them were nowhere to be found and never heard from again. They had disappeared into the dark recesses of the great mountain. They were swallowed whole—all of them; all of them except John. John was found about three quarters of a mile back from the mouth of the cave. Of course, he was dead. He died with a big smile on his face and a sack slung over his shoulder—a sack full of worthless, dirty rocks.

Of Blumhardt

One of the most devastating societal sicknesses our world has ever encountered has fooled us all. If there was something humans could call truth, it would be the most valuable commodity ever known to man. Regardless of what "truth" may actually be, the very notion that it could exist at all is enough for us to exploit that value for every lasting red cent. We call this social enterprise "religion."

Johann Christoph Blumhardt (1805–1880) was a Lutheran pastor from the Black Forest of Germany who proclaimed a radical overarching faith in Jesus Christ and demonstrated a living commitment to his coming kingdom. Yet his was a faith that transcended, abhorred even, pious religious platitudes. His commitment was to the objective reality of the reign of Jesus.

To Blumhardt, this disdain for religious piety was palpable and one of his enduring gifts of the Spirit was the ability to discern its malformed effects and tease out the inner realities of what it masks, especially in young people.

One young man, we'll call him Bobby, came to stay with Pastor Blumhardt and his family. On the surface, Bobby could easily have been categorized as a "disruptor," or a "troubled teen," but Blumhardt could see things from the boy's perspective, and get at the heart of his discord. While both saw religion as a charade, Blumhardt understood religion as simply a vaccine, the opiate that inoculates the people so they can't catch the real thing. Bobby, on the other hand, simply experienced it as getting a shot.

Pastor Blumhardt would keep a map of the world hung up on the wall. He would point to the map and tell all of his children and grandchildren, "Do you see that? All nations, the entire world, it all belongs to God and he reigns over all!" Put plainly, folks don't hear that enough in church. That's the difference.

Late one evening, long after everyone in the house had gone to bed, young Bobby snuck out into the common meeting room and grabbed one of the worship hymnals, took it out to the hen house, and threw it down in the fertile mixture of hay and chicken shit. He also took some of Pastor Blumhardt's papers and soaked them in the wash basin. And for good measure, he let the rooster loose in the meeting hall. Because why the hell not?

When the cock crowed the next morning, the women of the house (read: maids) came downstairs and were heartily greeted by the bird. They gave chase and, in an attempt to pin it down, were worked up into a wild frenzy. Bobby, who rose earlier than all of them, hid in one of the closets peering through a keyhole, doing everything he could to keep from laughing out loud.

One of the women found Pastor Blumhardt in his study and protested, "*Herr Pfarrer*! The boy has done it again! This time he put a hymn book in the hen house and now it's filthy! What are we going to do?"

Blumhardt couldn't help but chuckle. He totally got it.

"Dear lady, let it go, already! You'll give yourself a stroke with all this worry and anxiety! Besides that, deep down, I bet the absurdity of it tickles you pink! Let yourself smile, for once! Please, take a breath. I'll have one of the youngsters catch the rooster. As for the book, just toss it. The boy is surely worth a hymnal."

Shortly afterward, the entire household gathered together for breakfast. Bobby, expecting the worst, was completely disarmed when he sat down and not a word was spoken of his foolish pranks. From then on, he found better ways to get the Pastor's attention.

Interlude: At Bay

Long trips in the car with children yield two of the world's most profound questions: 'What time is it?' and 'Are we there yet?' The answers can be summed up *in Christ*: What time is it? It is the dawn of the new creation. Are we there yet? The old has gone and the new has come.

For those concerned that the gospel of Jesus Christ is being undermined by relativism: Good news is relative, depending on who receives it. For most, good news means, 'What's in it for me?' Our good news is being crucified with Christ.

What's so good about an instrument of death? If we weren't corrupt, this question would be moot. But once we consider what we're truly capable of, perhaps we'll wonder if even a cross will do the trick. Crucifixion to the old order keeps all our assumptions and biases at bay.

Why does Jesus say that unless you change and become like children, you won't enter the kingdom of God? Because children have to be told they are doing good or they won't realize it. We're biased towards believing in our good and assuming God will follow suit.

The Great Inversion

On the last day the great City of God finally opened its gates. All of the souls that lived for this moment were in queue. An angel stood guard at the gate, instructed to ask one simple question to all who would enter through: "What good is the good you do?"

As each soul answered, they either gained admittance or were turned away.

"I lived a pure and chaste life. I married and remained faithful to my spouse until the day I died."

"I lived a life in solidarity with the poor. I sold all my possessions and stored up treasures in heaven."

"I dedicated my life to fight for a healthy, just, sustainable, and equitable life for all. But especially for disproportionally affected communities of color."

The angel marveled at all the good that was done in the world. Many were surprised at the ease in which the angel let souls pass. Somewhere down the line, it even got to the point where all one had to do was listen in to the person in line ahead of them and then copy their answer—using different words, of course.

Some, however, were turned away. These were the few poor souls who either didn't have an answer or couldn't properly word a response. There were usually patches of silence, stammering, and occasionally some weeping. But most could give no answer, for they knew there was nothing that they could possibly say that could justify their presence in line.

Once the last soul had given their answer, time was ultimately thrown into the lake of fire. The gates of the city betrayed an eerie creak until they slammed to a final close. The word of God, once spoken, inviting, was now to be sealed in eternal silence.

Those on the outside were in utter darkness and a sudden chill climbed up their spines. All of those who had so confidently walked through the gates were actually, in their pride, exiting the great city. They assumed the good was the good they'd done. All of those who were broken before the Father were now gathered into his loving arms. They could scarcely tell what good they'd done, never mind what good it was. Their emptiness could only echo: "Why do you call me good?"

How Ability Shapes Society

Suppose there once was a king who had three sons. Every day these boys worked hard in the fields of his royal palace. One day, when the sun was at its highest point, their father drew near to them as they labored. The king was never seen in the fields, so when he appeared the three boys knew something was amiss.

He proclaimed, "My sons, my kingdom is in utter ruins. I need some time to draw up a strategy for governing our people. In the meantime, I am looking for the son who is willing to lead my people while I am away. But you will not be alone. You will always have our servants here to support you. You can always lean on them. And you have one another. There will be many trials and tests, much pain and suffering, but if you are faithful, you shall overcome. What say you? Which of you has the courage to restore my kingdom?"

The eldest son spoke up immediately. "Father," he said, "it is quite funny you should say this, for I have seen how the kingdom has taken a bad turn, and for the last five years I have been quietly making a plan to fix it all."

The eldest son relayed his entire plan, but just as he was giving his last words, his heart stopped beating and he dropped to the ground.

The middle son then spoke up. "Father," he said, "it would appear that my older brother will not be able to carry out his plan. He had many great thoughts, but I know how I can expand upon them and then the kingdom can be restored to even greater glory!"

He proceeded to tell of his better plan, and indeed, it was much better. However, just as he was giving his last words, his mind ceased to function properly and he fell down on all fours, barking like a dog. A rabbit darted by and off he went across the field to chase it. He was never heard from again.

The king looked down to his youngest son. The boy's eyes were turned downward as he tended his donkey.

"Speak, my boy."

The young boy, barely old enough to keep his bedroom in order, let alone the kingdom, finally whispered, "Father, I have no good thoughts or wise words to say. I have no powers or plans or abilities. I'm sorry, but I'm nobody."

The king had a thought, but said nothing aloud: "But you're my son. . ."

As much as the king hoped for his son to be heir apparent to the throne, he was also a realist. He nodded his head, turned around and began to walk away.

"But father," the youngest boy spoke up, "I can work with the servants and help them!"

The king raised an eyebrow.

"Thank you, son. I now know how to lead our people and restore the kingdom."

From that day forward, the king and his son worked alongside the servants, discovering their abilities, earning their trust, and all together, they upheld the affairs of their kingdom.

So could it be said: How we perceive ability sets us on a course of how we shape our world.

A Modern Caterpillar

One bright and happy morning a young caterpillar decided he wanted to go outside and play. He asked his mommy if it was okay and she said, "After you clean your room!" So, the young caterpillar cleaned up as fast as a caterpillar could and went out to play.

He thought it would be very fun to go find his very best caterpillar friend, but on his way, he encountered the most colorful creature he'd ever seen. He didn't know what it was or how to describe it, but it was way high up and it didn't walk on feet and it was yellow and orange and red and brown. It flipped and fluttered, dipped and danced, and continually circled just above the young caterpillar's head. He was thoroughly entranced!

He couldn't wait to tell his best friend about it, but when he got to his house, his friend wasn't there.

"Where could he possibly be?" the young caterpillar wondered. "He's always home at this time!" He didn't stick around to think about it for too long. In a flurry he was off again to see that beautiful flying dancer.

He couldn't find it again until he got all the way home, but once he arrived, there it was, flipping and dipping, fluttering and dancing right above his house. It was truly the neatest thing he'd ever seen! He just had to try it . . .

So the young caterpillar set out to find the prettiest, most colorful leaves he could. He searched all day, and when the sun had almost gone down, he finally found them. They were bright and brilliant—almost as beautiful as the flying dancer's.

Once he got his leaves, he scurried (as fast as a caterpillar can, anyway) to the maple tree and got some sap. Covering himself so he was nice and sticky, he gently placed the two leaves on his back. He thought it would be best to let it dry overnight.

The next morning, the caterpillar woke to the flying dancer fluttering overhead, but this time, he had his own brilliant wings too! Yet as much as he tried, he could not flip and flutter nor dip and dance. In fact, he couldn't even get off the ground.

How could he get up high? After lots of thinking and staring up in wonder at his new fluttering friend, he had an idea. He would climb up the stem of a rhododendron and wait for a bumblebee to come. Then he could hitch a ride!

So up he climbed and he waited for a good hour or two. When the bumblebee finally arrived, she was not happy to see the young caterpillar in her flower. She promptly stung him and sent him back to down to the ground. The leaves broke off of his back and he was covered in dirt and sticky sap.

The young caterpillar began to weep. He would never be able to flip, flutter, dip, or dance! There was simply nothing he could do to be like the beautiful flying dancer. Feeling very sad, he decided to forget all this and inch himself back home—and right into bed.

He was so sad but his bed felt so nice and comfortable. In no time at all he was fast asleep, and boy, oh boy, was it a deep sleep. The young caterpillar was so exhausted that he slept for an entire month!

Now, you'll never guess what happened when he woke up. He rose to the familiar sound of fluttering. He could hear the movement of someone dancing. He tried to open his eyes, but he saw nothing but bright colors—yellow, orange, red, and brown. Once he stepped out of bed, he gave a big yawn and an even bigger stretch—and whoosh! He was in the air—flipping and dipping, dancing, and, yes, fluttering! He was so happy that his little heart nearly burst with joy!

Then, just when he thought he could not get any happier, he heard the sound of his best friend calling to him, "Well, it's about time! I've been waiting for you! Let's go!" And off they flew, together again.

Ode to the Disappeared

A derelict beggar was holed up in a dark, dank abandoned breeze-way, perpendicular to a vacant alley. The dogs would pass him by, pretending not to see him, not wanting to be bothered. His prayers couldn't even turn the corner, drifting flatly and scraping the concrete, crumbling like a dead autumn leaf. Every great city has citizens that have suffered for its greatness.

This beggar was paralyzed from the waist down. Every day he would crawl with his arms, legs dragging behind him, leaving a wake of disagreement in the dust. His daily destination was the city gates, where he would prop himself up in his familiar post and hold up a small wooden bowl. Have you ever been a guest in someone's home and noticed the stacks of odds and ends stuffed in the corner? Oftentimes, it's the things we see every day that we wish weren't there that somehow seem to disappear.

"Grace and mercy! If not from God then from his people! Please have mercy!" The unkindly refrain was just off-putting enough to ease the conscience of most passers-by.

The man's position in society was secure, so long as it was secured in an upright position on the ground at the foot of the city gates. The standard offering was usually a pinch of rice, which, by day's end, could amount to half a bowl's worth. Upon quitting, he would drag himself back through his alley and turn the corner into the tucked away breezeway, where he would make a fire, cook his ration of rice, and eat. Every day he did this. Every day he would cry, "Grace and mercy!" to a culture capable of neither.

There was a morning he awoke, distinct in its color and luminescence. A pink haze infused the dawn. He thought he heard a bird or two. Off in the distance, there was definitely music. The thud of loosely tuned leather drums, the loopy whir of woodwinds, the arrogance of brass. What musters this joyful spectacle? The beggar dragged himself over to the gates to try and get a keener perspective on the matter, as well as his usual sampling of rice, but was surprised to find a caravan of people entering the city. There was singing. There was dancing. There was collective ego.

The beggar stretched his arms up and held his bowl up high. "Grace and mercy!" was definitively drowned out by the dervish decadence. Yet somehow the distinguished troop seemed not only to acknowledge the man, but to fixate on him. In indiscrete approach, they came close, smiled through their song, and dropped handfuls of rice in his bowl. A dozen or so followed suit, in the manner of ecstatic procession. In a matter of two minutes, he had accumulated enough rice to last him for the next three weeks.

At the end of the caravan, the music died. The presence of a grand coach annulled the activity, silently signifying a solemn finale. The visage of the dour beggar began to thaw as the King of the city took one stately step out onto a tread, the coach rocking and creaking, and then another. It was all a feverish illusion, fit for a tropical malady. In a moment of waking sleep paralysis, color draining from the beggar's face, he held up his bowl, hands seizing, expecting even more rice. The King drew near, and with a sober severity, said, "Beggar, give me your rice."

Nearing the climax of the dream, with every expectation of a rude awakening, the beggar felt his ashen face flush with a rush of blood to the head, with a tingling silence. He peered up at the King in horror.

Again, the King said, "Beggar, give me your rice."

The beggar nursed murderous thoughts. As if a cripple could combat a caravan. But a seething imagination harbors unimaginable ingenuity in violence. He clutched his bowl to his belly, looking up, peer becoming sneer. Few of us have been in a situation where we have, with all sincerity, completely given up hope. For anything. Utter malice and contempt for you, for me, for everyone I see. This was the state of the poor beggar. Handing over his rice wasn't as much an act of obedience as it was suicide. So he did what any self-respecting miserly coward would do. He pulled out three measly grains of rice and dropped them, slowly, one at a time, as if each one were an expletive, in the palm of the King's hand.

The King snapped his fingers, and an apprentice stepped out of the coach. A pathetic lad, really. He held in his hand three gold nuggets. He gently placed them on top of the beggar's overflowing rice bowl. Then the King and his apprentice got back into the coach and pulled away.

The music resumed, the procession marched on, and the already forgotten beggar wept with a stabbing regret. Even in his poverty, he was not truly poor.

(For D.D.)

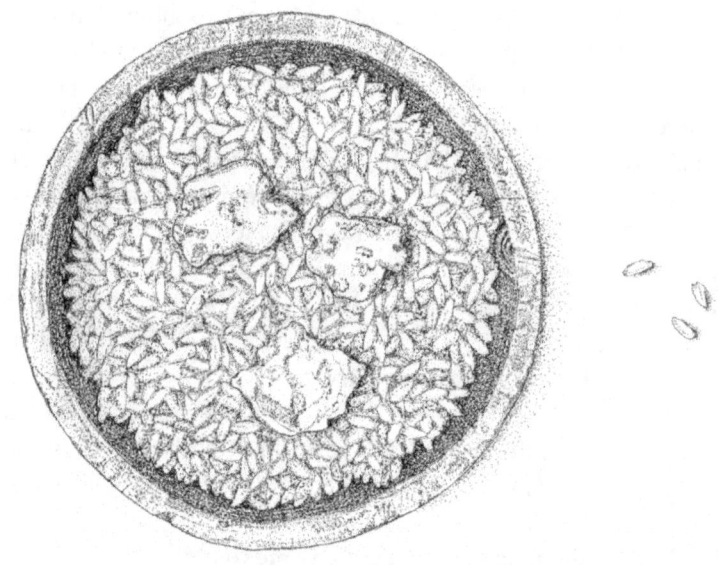

On Ashes and Masters

O God of the Air, consume me. All consuming
Master, teach me the knowledge of Thy ways.
In one mighty act, You are everywhere and
nowhere. How mighty, Thy invisible Hand
which stretches from one side of the globe to
the other, the interconnectedness that You
have established. May I never be found want-
ing. May my hands be ever employed, such
that my right hand doesn't know what my left
is doing. Yes, Lord, instruct me in Thy ways:
always longing, unquenching, ever reaching,
world without end. Amenable.

In the time of Cyrus the Persian there was a revered prophet in the
land named Daniel. Daniel was known for his faithfulness to the
God of the Hebrews. Cyrus and his disciples placed their devotion
at the feet of the one they called Bel, meaning "lord" or "master."

Bel was a statue made of clay encased in brass, which stood
alone in its own temple. Every evening, the worshippers of Bel
would enter the temple and lay lots of food and wine at its feet and
then leave, sealing the door behind them. When the king would go
to the temple each morning for his morning prayers, all of the food
and wine would be consumed. This was the sign that Bel was the
living God, worthy to be worshiped and revered.

One day Daniel and King Cyrus got into a discussion about who the true and living God really was. Daniel told the story of how his friends had been thrown into a fiery furnace and how his God was with them in the fire and they were spared. Cyrus retorted with the evidence of his daily devotions and how he could see with his own eyes how Bel consumed the food and the wine every night.

Evidently, he was not entirely convinced of his own argument, because eventually Cyrus decided that he had to know the truth—for sure. So he placed a challenge before Daniel. King Cyrus invited Daniel into the temple of Bel, as he himself would place the food and wine at its feet. He said, "Go home and return in the morning. If, upon your return, you find all of this food and wine consumed, you shall be banished from my kingdom. If not, we shall presume that Bel is a false god, and I will banish its worshippers instead." So Daniel agreed and stood by as the king laid the food at Bel's feet; and as the king stood by, Daniel scattered ash all over the floor of the temple. When they were both done, they sealed the door and left for the night.

The next morning, Daniel and Cyrus rose early and went to the temple together. When they arrived, the seal was not broken. Cyrus opened the doors and the two entered. There they saw all of the food and wine consumed. Cyrus began to laugh, but Daniel simply pointed to the floor.

The king was shocked. Sure enough, the footprints of many men, women, and children—the worshippers of Bel—were plainly visible in the scattered ash, and they all led to a little door hidden just behind the altar.

The divine right of today's king is confessed when we can no longer distinguish between church and commerce. Cornerstone. First. Community. Discover. Union. Mutual. Trust. Summit. Impact. Journey. Rock. Liberty. Memorial. Harvest. Covenant. These are today's footprints. Everywhere and nowhere. All-consuming. "Where can I go from your Spirit? Where can I flee from your presence?"

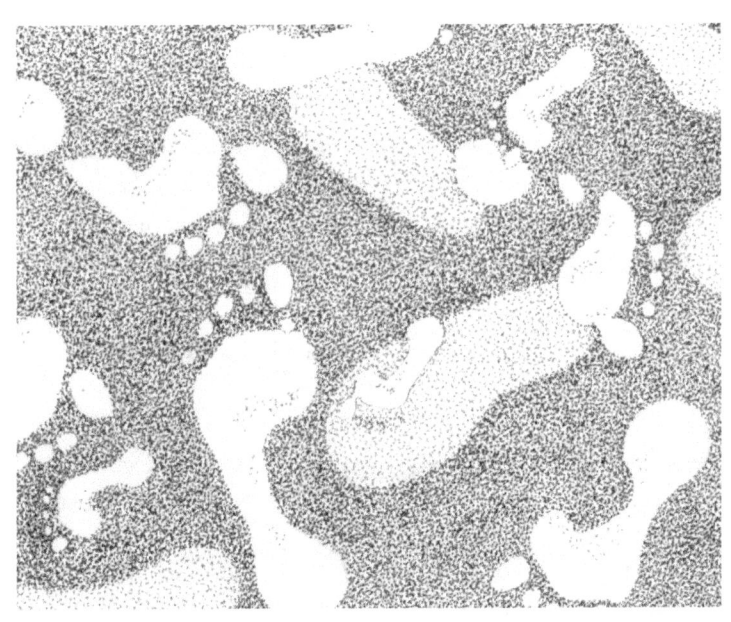

Minnesota Citrus

*Facts cannot be underestimated as they have
normative power. But they do not give us
insight into the truth, or the illumination of
poetry. Yes, accepted, the phone directory of
Manhattan contains four million entries, all of
them factually verifiable. But do we know why
Jonathan Smith, correctly listed, cries into his
pillow every night?*

-WERNER HERZOG ("MINNESOTA DECLARATION,
[SIX-POINT ADDENDUM]")

Once there were two orchards that sat side by side deep in Mid-western rural country. One was an apple farm and one was an orange grove.

The man who ran the apple farm was a just man. He paid his workers fair wages and their work was—appropriately—fruitful. It was not uncommon to hear the likes of singing, humming, whistling, laughter and dancing throughout the day.

The man who ran the orange grove, however, was a harsh man. He paid his workers little, and at times, he wouldn't pay them at all. The poor men and women that harvested oranges were sad and somber. The day was long and the work submerged them in a swallowing quiet.

One day an orange grove worker was picking oranges along the edge of the grove. As she worked up into a tree, she happened to peer over into the apple grove. She saw the singing and dancing. She

84

saw the joy and mirth. Sins and virtues both have a way of cascading. What would it matter to simply tag on envy?

It was shortly after that when the oranges began showing up at the apple orchard. At the end of the day, the accountants of the apples would take stock of everything that was harvested, and for some reason, they found oranges mixed in with all of the apples.

"How could this be?" they wondered. "Could an apple tree really produce oranges?" If you weren't clued in to the absurdity of this story, you should be good now.

The bewildered accountants went straight to the owner of the farm and reported what was happening. They worked themselves into quite a frenzy complaining about the oranges and how they don't belong.

The apple farmer remained calm and simply smiled. When the frantic accountants had finished airing out their concerns, he sat silently for a moment and then spoke:

"Did you know that my father buried the seeds for both of the orchards with his own two hands? He never intended for it to be this way. He never wanted them to be separate."

The accountants lowered their eyes to the floor.

The farmer continued, "The other day a woman from the orange grove approached me and told me about their horrible working conditions. I know the man who owns their operation and I know he's greedy and short-tempered. I told the poor woman to put her old life behind her and to come and work for me. So she did."

The accountants then scratched their heads and their eyes brightened. "Can we open another bank account—one for apple money and one for orange money?"

At this the owner of the apple tree grove became stern. "No! Apples are apples and oranges are oranges! Give to the apple farm what belongs to the apple farm and give to the orange grove what belongs to the orange grove!"

The accountants of the apples, realizing that they could not profit off of the oranges, tucked their chins and walked away.

Humanitarianism and it
Discontents

August 13, 2005. New York, NY.

An absurd tale: there was once a very poor man who lived in the Big Apple. He was very timid and shy and he had some friends, but he did not have a home. His friends were more outgoing. This meant that they begged more, and because of this, they always got more money and food.

On this summer afternoon, the poor man worked up enough courage to stop the next man he saw walking by with a suit on. He said to him, "Sir, I have a question for you. I do not want any of your money or any other handouts. I was just wondering if you would switch clothes with me for one hour. I cannot beg, for I am very afraid of people. I wish this wasn't so, but my story is long and sad, and I have been hurt very deeply. Perhaps you could gather alms, and I could walk the streets with dignity for a little while."

The man in the suit happened to be a Christian man. He was raised to believe that he should always lend a hand, but from a business perspective, he always thought that panhandlers had it all wrong. He figured he could double the poor man's money in one hour. The ghost of Holy Scripture haunted him, something along the lines of what you do to the least of these. He would've taken Jesus off the cross if he could.

"Sure," the man replied, almost giddy for the opportunity. "Knock yourself out!"

The two men ducked into an alley. The man with the suit had already calculated that his undershirt and shorts could actually pass for leisure gear, so he feigned humility in refusing to receive the poor man's tattered rags.

"No, really, it's okay. I'll be fine. You go ahead and take my clothes, and I'll stick around here for a while. You'll notice there's also the dignified scent of cologne and a bit of aftershave. Really, take your time. There's also a little something inside the jacket pocket. Get yourself something nice while you're at it."

The poor man, after receiving assistance tying the tie, tugged at the front of the sport coat and did not release his grip as he lifted his chin and began to walk around the block.

The benefactor remained in the alley, observing from a distance. While he sure felt good that the poor man felt empowered, he contemplated just taking off, so as to surprise the man with the gift of abandonment and an expensive suit. Once again, he reassured himself about his gift to the least of these, and was briefly haunted by the second half of that verse, but did not linger long enough for it to pierce him. He began to sneak away, keeping an eye on the poor man.

The poor man was thoroughly enraptured by the scent of masculine elegance that continued to waft from the sport coat. He lifted the front of it up above his face to breathe it in deeply, as if he were siphoning off the wealth. He had closed his eyes so as to absorb more sense through his nose when the screech of tires and a swift knock at the knees sent him upside down and face first onto the hot pavement, black sport coat pulled up over his head like a chastened hockey player.

Our benefactor stood frozen, about two blocks away. All at once, the second half of verse forty rushed his thoughts: "You do unto me." He did not know if the man was dead, and frankly, there was not even so much as a spark of courage present to go and find out. He had nailed this man to the tree. His suit was ruined. And the sight of Christ crucified was so pathetic that it just pissed him off. He tossed the poor man's cup of change in the street, got in his car, and drove away.

Beaver! Don't Lose Heart!

Beaver was having a moment. With eyes locked forward and vision out of focus, he pondered life and what it all meant. He considered all of the creatures in the world, the fierce and the lonely, the mighty and the hurting. "Dear God. . ." he whispered to himself, mostly in vain, but with a slight possibility of prayer. As ponderings led him into a rabbit hole of power, politics, and the prison industrial complex, reality began to sink its teeth in and his heart began to beat faster.

Beaver's sadness and sense of the tragic became impossibly heavy and imperceptibly oppressive. On the outside, he remained a thoroughbred brown beauty, a rare sight in the forest, indeed. But on the inside, with his keen sense of the world's worsening wrongness, he was holding onto his last hints of hope.

When in the midst of despair, sometimes we can all defer to the soothing silences of sleep. Beaver was no exception.

It came upon him in a dream state, although completely awake and aware, or so he dreamt. Maybe it was the pitifulness of his prayer. But it weighed on him like a wet pile of leaves. He was shown a vision of the biggest dam in the world—big enough to stop up all the tears that have been shed throughout the world. The still water glistened like glass, and Beaver watched himself, in out-of-body fashion, proudly sitting atop this unparalleled marvel of nature.

With the startling snap of a cosmic finger, he awoke. The chaotic silence of the deep woods: birds, insects, slight branches dropping, the crackle of leaves. The setting was all too familiar. But within, nothing was the same. Beaver resolved to build that dam.

He began chomping away, and he felled the first few trees easily. Even he was surprised by his stamina. Other beavers from adjacent dens observed the spectacle. Some cheered while others scratched their heads (carefully, as their claws can be quite sharp). Hours went by and the enthusiasm began to wear off. The crowd thinned, and with them went the encouragement.

It was at about his fiftieth tree when one of his two front teeth came right out of his mouth. Aside from the debilitating depression and despair, it was the most painful thing he'd ever experienced. Overcome with emotion, he lay on his back, gripping his mouth, looking up above him to the towering trees that still stood overhead, and realized he was going to fail.

At this point, the story gets blurry. Beaver may have gone into shock. He most definitely began to hallucinate, or at minimum, he passed out from the pain. And within, the dreams do not relent.

Beaver observed himself from above lying helplessly on the forest floor. Then, he felt himself flutter down, slowly, gently, with a reassuring rhythm. He was a leaf. He sensed the arms of God in the form of a balanced breeze, until he touched down upon his own nose. Returning to his own beaver body, he sat up to read the message that was scrawled upon the leaf. It was a moment of utter self-realization in the form of failure and weakness. But as he read the message, the pain in his mouth went away, or at least he forgot about it:

> *Beaver! Don't lose heart! The way of the tree is stillness. We are not frantic and we are not anxious, but we sustain life in all creatures. Our roots run deep and together we are slowly grounded firmly in place. How did we get here? By the seed of those who have gone before us. It drops, it dies, and new life sprouts. Beaver! Don't lose heart! The way of the tree is stillness.*

Advent, Etc.

It happened one day in the heavens that the Master gave direction to the angel Gabriel saying, "Walk upon the Earth as a man. Sweep its entire surface, looking high and low for signs of the peace I have promised. Who will be found faithful?"

So the angel Gabriel took leave from heaven and appeared on Earth in the form of a poor wanderer. Knowing that men tended to congregate, he decided to first visit the major cities. To his surprise, he found that everywhere he went love and peace were on the lips of almost everyone. He was greatly encouraged as he saw families constantly tell each other, "I love you." He saw large mobs of people gathering together chanting together and holding signs for peace. He saw people feeding and giving alms to hundreds upon thousands of poor people. More cities were being developed and neighborhoods were being transformed. So much good was being done in the world, much of it even bearing the name of the Master.

Every city he went to was the same. Signs of peace, love, and justice were everywhere.

"The Master is going to be so pleased!" he thought.

Gabriel had barely taken his leave when he noticed that despite all the good that humans were doing, there was a web covering the Earth that tied them all to a particular way of perceiving, knowing, and interacting. They could only take the good with the bad. And someone's good was always another's bad. It was a moral hall of mirrors.

The angel gasped in horror. It was as if the shades were raised and the curtain torn. He saw through the many words and the noise of the crowds, into the hearts of all who spoke of "peace, peace," but of which there was none at all. He recognized the work of an enemy feverishly spinning webs of global enslavement. It was all they could do because the Earth itself belonged to the Master. Deeply disturbed, Gabriel took leave of the Earth as fast as he could and fell at the feet of his Master, weeping.

"What can be done, my Lord? They've taken all that you've given and learned to twist it for their own gain! Love, they've taken for good feelings. Peace, they've used to justify separation. Justice, they've harnessed for the sake of accumulating power for themselves!"

The Master leaned over and whispered into the ear of the angel, thereby giving him enough strength and courage to continue his task.

Gabriel then returned to Earth, aiming for the gaps in the webs of globalization. He came upon the small towns and villages of the unlearned. He entered into the economically disadvantaged communities. He was welcomed by the scattered and marginalized.

It was a cry for help and the response of loved ones that allowed him to perceive the first real sign of peace: A baby, gasping its first breaths, born of a widowed mother in a run-down farm house. It reminded Gabriel of the gentleness of the virgin birth in Bethlehem on that first Christmas so long ago.

Gabriel continued on, seeking another sign. He went no further than the next house. Here, an old man sighed. His whole family gathered around him and offered up prayers to the Master. He breathed his last. Gabriel cracked a smile as he watched the man take leave of Earth.

The third sign came right away. It was the next house on the same street. Here, a gathering of ten or twelve men and women were gathered around a table. Their home was joyful and merry, yet with reverence and respect. They spoke mostly of their neighbors— the expecting widow and the dying old man—but their thoughts reached out over the entire world. They recognized the coming of the Master and they looked for him right in their midst.

Gabriel knew he had found what he was looking for. In small pockets around the globe, women and men surrendered to the invasive movement of God's Spirit, despite the web of illusion being woven. Here was no grand effort of mankind. Rather, it was the simple hope of a single woman. It was the poor sigh of a man giving his life. It was the joyful expectancy of a gathered household.

For those with ears to hear.

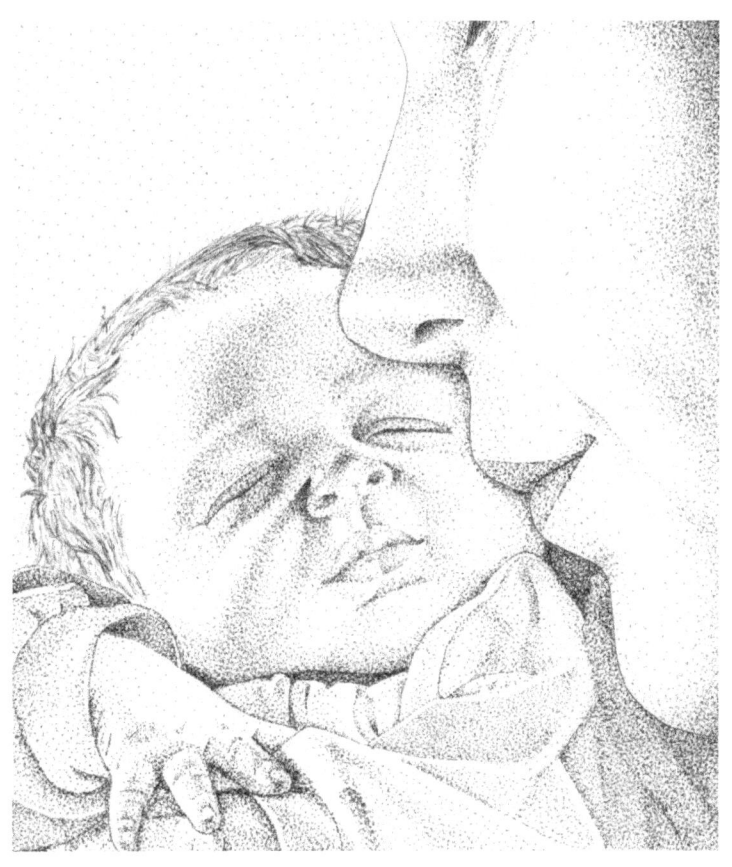

A Trinity of Denial

One day Noah, Job, and Daniel were working together in the fields of eternity reflecting on the virtues given to them by God. Noah possessed nothing. Job suffered tribulation faithfully. Daniel discerned rightly in the presence of the king.

Suddenly, Peter appeared before them and they were thunderstruck at the sight of this simple fisherman. Here was one that denied the Lord not once, not twice, but three times. A trinity of denial.

Noah, Job, and Daniel could scarcely approach the man. They could not fathom the depths of one illumined by forgiveness.

A Modern Woman
(Caught in the Sin of Adultery)

"No judgment," she said.
   "No judgment," they said.
   No one noticed the rocks on the ground. Or Jesus.

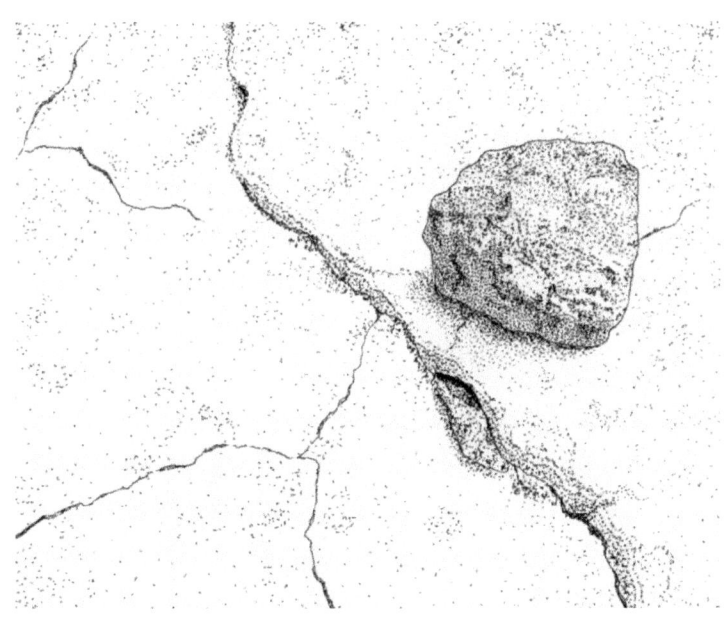

The Cat, the Dog, and the Master

The cat was walking through the front yard of a house he had long shared with the family dog. He knew the look on the dog's face meant there was something on the tip of his tongue.

"What are you grinning at?" he asked the dog.

"Nothing much," retorted the dog, who had a silly grin plastered on his face. "It's just that my Master is very pleased with me."

"Oh yeah, why's that?" inquired the cat.

"Because I do my Master's will."

"Oh, do you?"

"Yes, in fact, I do. When my Master tells me to sit, I sit. When my Master tells me to roll over, I obey. When my Master tells me to heel, I do it."

"Very good. But I see that you are attached to that tree stump over there. Is that your Master's will as well?"

Knowing where the cat might be going with this, the dog became defensive. "Yes, obviously it is my Master's will that I be tied up or I wouldn't be here. And as you see, I am perfectly fine with it. I'm not complaining, barking, whining or anything.""I see, I see. So if I were to just chew through that leash for you, would you continue to do your Master's will?" Presently, the cat began to gnaw through the leather strap. The dog began to get nervous.

"Stop that! Hey, stop chewing that! You're gonna get me in trouble!"

Once the cat had chewed all the way through the leash, essentially liberating the dog, he proclaimed, "I also obey. Only I do so because I am bound to our Master, not to a stump."

The dog, unable to control his animal urges, put his nose to the ground and was unable to lift it back up. Instead of following the will of his Master, it turned out that he was bound to the will of his nose. The cat stood by as the dog wandered off, never to be seen again.

Thomas the Apostle
is Exiled to India

Years after the day of Pentecost, the apostles Peter, James, and John went on to become pillars of the church in Jerusalem. Meanwhile, doubting Thomas found himself wondering, "Why couldn't I be the rock of the church like Peter?"

With his eyes turned low and his bearded chin wagging, he literally ran right into Jesus, who had suddenly appeared in his path. "Rabbi! Is it really you?" he questioned.

"Fear not, Thomas! Go to India and give them my gospel of peace."

Thomas replied, "Rabbi, if it truly be your will, show me a sign!" And with that Jesus was gone.

Three days later, Thomas again found himself mulling about. "Why couldn't I be the brother of our Lord like James?"

He was so wrapped up in his own thoughts that he again ran head-long into Jesus who had appeared in his path. "Rabbi! Is it really you?" he inquired.

"Thomas, be not afraid! Go to India and deliver to them my gospel of hope."

Thomas replied, "Rabbi, if it truly be your will, then make a way!" And with that Jesus was gone.

Three days later still, feeling more discouraged than ever, Thomas was wandering about aimlessly complaining, "Why couldn't I be the disciple Jesus loved like John?"

It was then that he bumped into Jesus for a third time. "Rabbi! It's not you, is it?" he wondered.

Jesus spoke, "Perfect love casts out fear! My beloved Thomas, go to India and preach the gospel of salvation."

Thomas's stubbornness was finally beginning to clear up but before he could even begin to muster a response, Jesus was gone. Then suddenly, three men in dark tunics overcame him with a blindfold and rope and carried him off, sold like a slave to an Indian king.

And so the story goes: God's mission breaks in on the world not through our strategies and strength, but through our weakness of will and clouds of doubt.

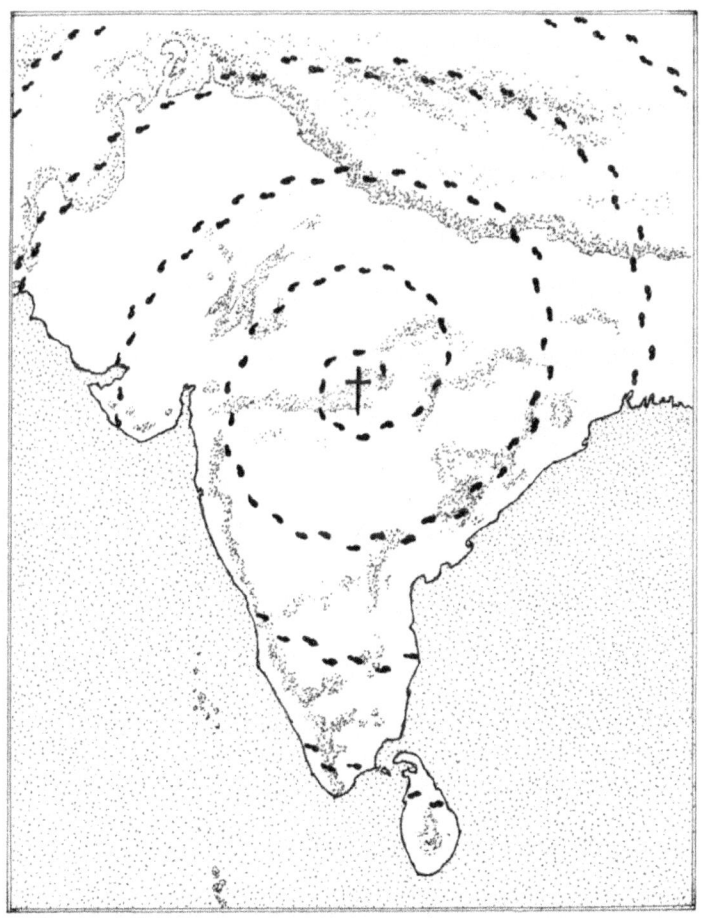

The Deer, the Bunny,
and the Locust

Once upon a time a man left family, home and work to lead the simple life of a barefoot wanderer. He had become thoroughly disillusioned with the world and its gluttony and greed. So he forsook all natural desires and pleasure, swearing off everything from modern transportation and medicine to entertainment and eating meat. He was especially against eating meat.

Once he set off, he told himself that he would simply trust the good Lord for his daily bread. He would obviously not hunt and certainly not beg. He thought, "God knows of my needs before I even ask." It was about the third day of a strict fast when a deer happened upon the trail he was walking. "My, oh my," thought the man. "What beauty!"

The deer fixed his gaze upon this strange gentleman with no shoes on. The man stared back for a few minutes, smiled lightly, and walked on. Watching him disappear into the horizon, the deer shook his head and said to himself, "For shame. The man is starving, and he must be blind as well!" Grateful for another day to prance about, the deer skipped off.

On the fifth day of the fast, the man nearly tripped over a slumbering bunny. "How peculiar," thought the barefoot man. "What bunny would allow itself to be overcome by a man?" Upon closer inspection, he murmured, "What beauty!" to himself, and carried on.

The bunny sat up and said, "Stupid man! I've been sent for the satisfaction of this foolish man, and he does nothing but stare at me! What shall I tell my Master?" Grateful for another day to hop about, the bunny charged off.

After a full week of fasting, the man accidentally stepped on a locust. Immediately, he attacked himself with guilt and grief, and nearly wept for the unfortunate insect. Tempted with hunger pangs, he began to think of John the Baptizer, who in the wilderness ate locusts and honey. Staring down at the bug, the man thought to himself, "What beauty! John the Baptizer, who was unworthy to untie the sandal of our Lord . . . in the same respect am I unworthy to eat in his manner." He dug a small hole six inches deep, buried the locust, and said a small prayer, thinking it had a soul like a man. He then crossed himself and walked on.

As the bug lay in the ground, it spoke aloud, "Master, I too have offered myself up for your child, according to your good pleasure, but this child of yours is led astray by the many idols he has placed before you. Have mercy on him and on all of us, unworthy of the honor of sacrifice!"

The Dream of the Monkey

Once, there was a zoo that had every kind of animal you could think of: lions, tigers, horses, bears, lemurs, frogs, peacocks, lizards, eagles, you name it. Days went by slowly for the animals, but it helped to see the peoples' faces light up as they walked by. Everybody especially loved the children.

Now, in this zoo, there was a certain monkey. This monkey lived among other monkeys in the very center of the zoo and he observed everything around him very closely. As happy as everything always seemed to be, he knew deep down that there was something very wrong.

One night, this monkey had a dream. In the dream, a great sheet descended from the heavens and on that sheet, he saw all his friends from the zoo: the lions, the lemurs, the tigers, the elephants—everybody was there. But there was one major difference. There were no cages. Everyone was able to roam and graze and play. The people were there, too, and they were able to pet and feed and play with all the animals. This was a dream where all creatures lived in a single, unified kingdom and there were no enemies or divisions. The lion would lay down with the lamb and the deadly snakes would play with the children.

When the monkey awoke, he looked around and even though he saw the joy of the children and heard the occasional laughter of the hyena, it was now perfectly clear to him what was missing.

All the attention turned to the primate exhibit when our wise old monkey began to cause a stir. He stood upright, gripped the bars of his cage and began screeching and squawking the prophetic message of the coming Animal Kingdom.

Since most of the other creatures in the zoo could not speak or understand monkey, they just stood back and laughed at the poor primate's penetrating eyes and ecstatic conviction. Those who could understand monkey, however, heard a message of good news that shook them to their very core. That night, when all the other animals were asleep, the monkeys unlocked and opened all of the cages in the entire zoo. Some animals chose to leave their habitats and others remained.

In the morning, the zookeepers discovered the anarchy and knew immediately who was to blame. They apprehended the wise old monkey and his cohorts, who were never heard from again.

The Sea Sections

. . . knowing that a man is not justified by
the works of the law, but by the faith of Jesus
Christ, even we have believed in Jesus Christ,
that we might be justified by the faith of
Christ, and not by the works of the law: for by
the works of the law shall no flesh be justified.

-GALATIANS 2:16 (AV)

They say he wasn't overly pious, as popes go. Not really the type to sport crisp white linens. For preaching a gospel of disruption, Saint Clement was banished to hard labor in the salt mines of Crimea, surrounded by hundreds of darkened, unforgiving souls. For Clement, the gospel was simply that: good news. Everything else was ornamental and in vain.

These men, his fellow prisoners, were hoarse, coarse, and horny. Their language blue enough to make you red. But even they couldn't make this pope blush. He simply lived and worked among them. Truly good news helps you understand the subtleties and absurdities of a world in folly. If it weren't so tragic, it would be truly hilarious. Grumble and gossip, tell a joke and take a piss, what else is there to do in a salty void? The truly delirious would do nothing but lick the walls. The Roman Empire wasn't looking for a data dump of salt extraction numbers. The salt mines were essentially a death sentence.

But good news is good news. Forget transformation. This is a story of transfiguration. In the end, death doesn't win, but it is the protagonist that unlocks the meaning of resurrection. The question was, what good is good news when you're stuck with the rocks in a hard place, when you can no longer tell the difference between salivation, salvation, and salination? Clement could only speak of a power that was unleashed at the decisive event of Christ's death. He talked about carrying around the death of Christ in his own body.

Over time, this gospel message would take root in the caves. But as our Lord prophesied, it found soil in all manner of shape and stink. Even today, we want our good news with a cherry on top. But Clement couldn't shake the cross of Jesus Christ. This is precisely where most men began to stumble over the message. "Take your good news and shove it," is the toned-down translation. "Enough death already! Give us liberty or give us life. You can keep the rest." The more hopeful and optimistic would try to reason with our pope. "Clement, brother, you've got it all wrong. Our hope is not in Jesus' death. It's in his resurrection! It's in eternal life!" As if their current lot in life was a mere abstraction.

Others had no problem with this Jesus story, one way or the other. Only, they managed to reduce it to a moral philosophy. To them, what mattered was what Jesus taught, the life he lived, and how. The cross of Jesus could simply be reduced to: *deny yourself.* Of course, Clement did not object to this. He said it only told half the story. "There's more to life than being right." Especially if that right is good, pure, and holy. That's a pretty isolating existence in this world of thievery and prostitution, economic or otherwise. As some brothers would repent, they would become bent on the imitation of the ethical Christ. Clement warned that this was a yoke they could not and must not carry. Rather, cross-shaped imitation is no more than a life lived in freedom from the enslaving powers that have been emasculated and exposed; and of course, with the blow-back that comes with the cost. And besides, what good would the moral life be for these salty miners? The taste of salt covered their tongues. Its touch clogged their pores. This was all they had left to live for. And the irony of it—here they were surrounded by salt, a preservative, but no one knew what they were being preserved for. Therefore, the good news would await its transfiguration in their midst.

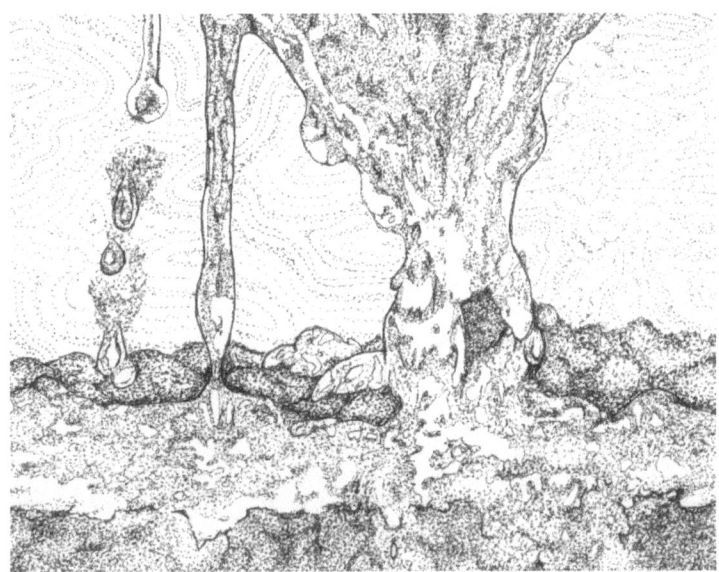

To Clement, the good news of the cross of Jesus was all about exposure. Revelation, you could say, at risk of more religion. Better, invasion. "The world as we know it, the one that put us here among the rocks, has been undone. Listen and you will hear: the rocks cry out! Beneath the rubble, your hearts cry out! These are the signs of hope. Do not snuff them out. Therefore, the task is: Discern, discern, discern!"

Once, a man came to Clement under the darkness of night, an odor of shame wafting from his soul. He said, "Brother, I came to the mines as a Christian, but I fear I am losing my faith!"

St. Clement, incredulous, responded thus: "In the words of the great Karl Barth, who ever told you it was yours to lose?"

And the bleaker things got, the more the questions came. "How do you find the strength to go on? What is this good news? How can we have faith?"

The pope leveled with them all: "Brothers, I don't have a faith. Jesus has faith enough for us all. Can we accommodate him?"

And so, once the men began to lay down their goodness and moralities, a fresh breeze of change moved in, and even more than that, a gush of fresh water was miraculously released from the salty stones in the walls of the mine. Like the water from the rock, the water from Christ's pierced side, it was the sure sign of life they were looking for.

This would be a great ending to the story, if it were the ending. Once the Roman Empire got wind of the new allegiances that had broken into the caves, they abducted the instigator. They took our pope and tied him to a watery cross, tossing him headlong into the Black Sea. Once again, the cross of Christ echoed throughout history in a fractal pattern like cosmic sonar.

Years later, the waters of the sea parted, revealing a tomb prepared by the angels themselves.

Antinomies of the Dark Cloak

It was the time of the annual festival and a poor family from Nazareth was trekking across the wilderness. Along the way, the family was tested three times by a man who was completely shrouded in a dark black cloak.

Each time, he appeared suddenly, like a thief or a bee sting, always uninvited. When he drew near, an ominous chill rattled the spines of the children. His voice was low and hushed, his face merely a black hole obscured by the looseness of the fabric.

The first encounter was quite frightful, for the man seemingly arose from the ground. A mighty wind had kicked up some sand into a loosely formed funnel cloud, and behold, the dark cloak took shape. The children all found their places behind the mother and father, and each peeked through a body part to get a glance: over an elbow, between the legs, around the waist, over the shoulder. The Cloak held out both arms, as if to make an offering. Hands remained obscured.

"The Law or Faith: choose wisely and you shall pass."

The mother reasoned that this journey itself was act of faith made out of their poverty. As she inched forward towards the Cloak, the eyes of his children, glazed over, stared up at her. Her shoulders broadened and she proudly proclaimed, "It is by Faith alone!"

Thunder pealed and the family passed through.

The second encounter, while less disorienting, was no less disturbing. The children came out from hiding, yet each held on to an article of their parents' clothing. Again, the Cloak held out his arms.

"Grace or Works: choose wisely and you shall pass."

The father was schooled by the wisdom of generations of families descended from the kin of the Nazarene carpenter. He knew

well the theologies to uphold and the ones to avoid. In his mind, the answer was crystal clear. "It is by Grace alone!"

Streaks of snake lighting lit up the horizon, the belly of the earth rumbled calmly, and the family passed through.

By the third encounter, the children had been on the lookout for the Cloak. So when he appeared, they were ready. A mere mile later, the wind kicked up again, and like a phoenix, the dark cloak arose from the desert sand.

"Is it by Faith alone or is it by Grace alone: Choose wisely and you shall pass." The mother and the father turned to face each other, as if in a stalemate. No one present took notice of the youngest of the children. She reached out and playfully gave a tug on the hem of the dark Cloak. She felt it give a little and pulled again. As she continued to pull, the dark Cloak began to unravel until it was completely laid flat before them. In its place stood a tiny, dried-up bush.

All at once, thunder and lightning crashed, setting the bush aflame. Looking down in awe, the family marveled at how it did not burn up. Then, God spoke from within the bush.

"Neither faith nor grace is anything. Behold, a New Creation!"

Razed to New Life

"*What sort of good* is the good we do?" The question keeps haunting me.

"There's a reason clouds are gray," she said.

"Where are you going?" I said.

"It's a lofty world of black and white," she said. "And good and bad."

"Mother, tell me a story beyond them both."

"There was once a kingdom under siege and engulfed in flames. Citizens cried and screamed, fleeing in every direction while arsons torched the whole town. What is the good to be done now? You nurse burn victims while the kingdom crumbles. You take out the terrorists, enacting more torture tactics. You douse flames while the people perish. You tell them, 'It's gonna be okay,' lies appropriate to the pit of hell that they're in. What sort of good is this?"

"Relative," I said.

"But there's a king in this kingdom. He's spotted running against the grain of escapees, like a boy at the beach aiming for the waves, straight into the towering inferno. What good is the good we do? Silence smothered the city like a wet blanket soaking up sobs and tears. Hours went by as the people fell to their knees, mourning and weeping in disbelief. The day itself joined in lament as the sun also bowed down in humble reverence to the darkness. The people remained in place while the castle was reduced to a smoldering pile of gray ash. Is the fire good?" she riddled.

"Relative," I riddled in return, "Is he resurrected?"

"Sure," she said. "But resurrection itself is still relative. Let the king's life go. The town, the terrorists, and the tortured are all transfigured."

For those with eyes to see, I guess.

The Great Subversion

Once the last soul had given their answer, time was ultimately thrown into the lake of fire. The gates of the city betrayed an eerie creak as they slammed to a final close. The word of God, once spoken, inviting, was now to be sealed in eternal silence.

Those on the outside were in utter darkness and a sudden chill climbed up their spines. All of those who had so confidently walked through the gates were actually, in their pride, exiting the great city. They assumed the good was the good they'd done. All of those who were broken before the Father were now gathered into his loving arms. They could scarcely tell what good they'd done, never mind what good it was. Their emptiness could only echo: "Why do you call me good?"

"Why do you call me good? Why do you call me good?" The echo reverberated in what was meant to be eternal silence. The emptiness began to take on a messianic ring. It became apparent to them that God was on their side. They feasted upon death together as the sign of the possession they fulfilled for the entire world.

Then suddenly, the ground of the Great City split wide open, tearing apart the gates, creating a gaping chasm that yawned between the in and the out. A sea of fire cascaded from the clouds above, setting the atmosphere ablaze, waves of solar rays casting them all into blindness, yet revealing the truth. Whereas the torrent from the heavens set Noah and his family apart, this fiery baptism put everyone in the same boat. The scandal of the cross reveals the violence of our goodness.

The Boy Named King

They called the boy King. They called the boy King because that's his name. They named him King, but he never took to ruling. He said he couldn't rule because he wasn't king. They just called him King. Because that's his name. But what's in a calling?

As far as rulers go, the boy would make a terrible king. He's just a boy. He's just a boy they called King because that's his name. Boy, a king in name only would make a terrible ruler. A king in name only would make a terrible king. But what's in a name?

As far as King goes, the boy would make an interesting ruler. He's just a boy. He's just a boy they call King. But what if, *just what if,* they would name the boy king? That would be interesting. He never took to ruling. But is he called to be a king? What's in the boy?

As far as kings go, the boy would make a just king. Just kidding. But what if? What if I wasn't kidding? Boy, it would be interesting to see a king who never took to ruling. What kind of king is that? What if that king was called? He's just a boy named King named king. He's the boy they called a just king who never took to ruling.

Even as a boy, King would imagine his kingdom. When King was named king, he drew a map without borders. His kingdom had no borders. His kingdom knew no end. This kingdom was called just. This kingdom named an interesting king who never took to ruling. King was a terribly interesting boy. But an even more interesting king.

Kings draw maps with lines. King drew maps with colors. A king cannot layer his lines, but King contoured his kingdom by colors. King was just a boy, but he would make a terribly just king. How could his kingdom know no end? How could King be called

king if he never took to ruling? How could King be king if his kingdom had no lines?

The boy says: these colors run deep.

I wrote a letter to the king. I wrote to King because I wanted
to see in color. I wrote to the boy because I was terribly interested
to see a just kingdom where the king never took to ruling. I wanted
to see a kingdom without borders. I wanted to see a kingdom with
a boy king that knew no end.

I wrote a letter to the boy. I wrote a letter to the boy because
I was terribly interested. I was so interested that I couldn't sleep. I
couldn't sleep for a week.

When I can't sleep, I dream. I dream of a different kingdom.
I dream of a different kingdom with a different king. It is a terrible kingdom. It is a terrible kingdom with lots of lines. It is a terrible kingdom that isn't just. Just kidding. I am awake. And it is a
nightmare.

The different king said: these colors don't run.

As far as letters go, how long does it take to reach a kingdom
without borders? How long does it take to get to a kingdom that
knows no end? A second week of no sleep and no response and
doubts began to creep. Maybe the king sees that my maps are deeply
political.

As far as borders go, I began to doubt the just king and I began
to doubt a kingdom that knew no end and I began to doubt a kingdom with a boy for a king. I began to draw lines on my map with
a ruler. It was different and it was terrible and it was a nightmare.

As far as week three goes, I was greeted with a letter and
granted sleep.

I began to dream in color. I was awake.

Come and see.

-King

Of Swordplay

Along a golden pathway on the way to the king, I encountered his jester. He came entirely too close to my face.

"What's your pleasure, good sir?" I said.

"Ah, thanks for asking!" he said. "I enjoy long walks on the beach and cool evenings by the fire!"

"No, I mean, can I help you?" I said.

"Why, sure! Here, hold this," he said, handing me his sword.

"Never mind," I said, handing it back. "You've heard the words of Jesus, haven't you?"

"Of course!" he said. "I did not come to bring peace but a sword! So there you go." He gave it back to me.

"Oh, I can play this game," I said. "Here, the sword helps those who helps himself." Once more I gave it back.

"Good," he said as he sheathed it. "'Cause in the beginning was the sword, and the sword was with God, and the sword was. . . "

"Now, now, don't be a blasphemer."

"Are you pulling my leg?" he said.

I let out a thigh.

"You're a knee slapper!" he said.

"You're just gonna keep going down, I have a notion."

"Ha! I have-a no ankles. It's why I walk like this."

I can't really describe his jelly leg dance.

"I know what you're thinking," he said. "Something strange is afoot."

"Ah," I said. "Maybe he helps toes who help themselves."

"Well, they told Jesus, 'Physician, heal thyself. But he didn't! That's the bottom line. That's the good news of the king!" I nodded in agreement and he continued, "I like you. You're a down-to-earth guy."

We began to walk the road together.

"Yeah, you're a fun guy," I said, admiring the orange, pink, green, and glitter.

"There's a mushroom, alright, but that didn't stop you from getting into my face!"

"Excuse me?" I quipped. "You got in my face first!"

"Listen, if you wanna go face-first," he said, "I can help you with that."

He tripped me.

"Oh, shitake!" I said. I got up and brushed myself off. "You're quite a goof, aren't 'cha?"

"Why, yes, orange and pink and green and glitter."

"Are you going to join me to the king?" I asked.

"Ah, sorry, the king would like to keep his body to himself."

"I mean, will you follow me?"

"Ah, another quote from Jesus? 'I'll make you fishers of men!' Yes sir, I'm quite a catch!"

"Right, of course you are. What I meant to say earlier was, 'Those who live by the sword die by the sword!' Tell me of your kingdom."

"What is it you're looking for? You tell me that and I'll tell you if we have it. But I'll tell you now that we don't, so don't bother about that," he said, "Don't tell me about what it is you're looking for."

Disregarding his antics, I said, "I imagine a city on a hill. I imagine a kingdom without violence. I imagine a church as a *polis*."

"Why would you want that? You're American! You can keep your kielbasa."

"I'm seeking the politics of Jesus," I said.

"Why would you want that? You're American! You can keep your politics."

I stopped walking.

He continued, "Forget what you're seeking. And do not rely on your imagination, as it is still held captive. That you would rely on your own imagination tells me you haven't yet discerned your own captivity."

He stopped walking.

"A kingdom without violence. Well, I have a poem for you."

The jester proceeded to unsheathe his sword and shove it straight down his own throat.

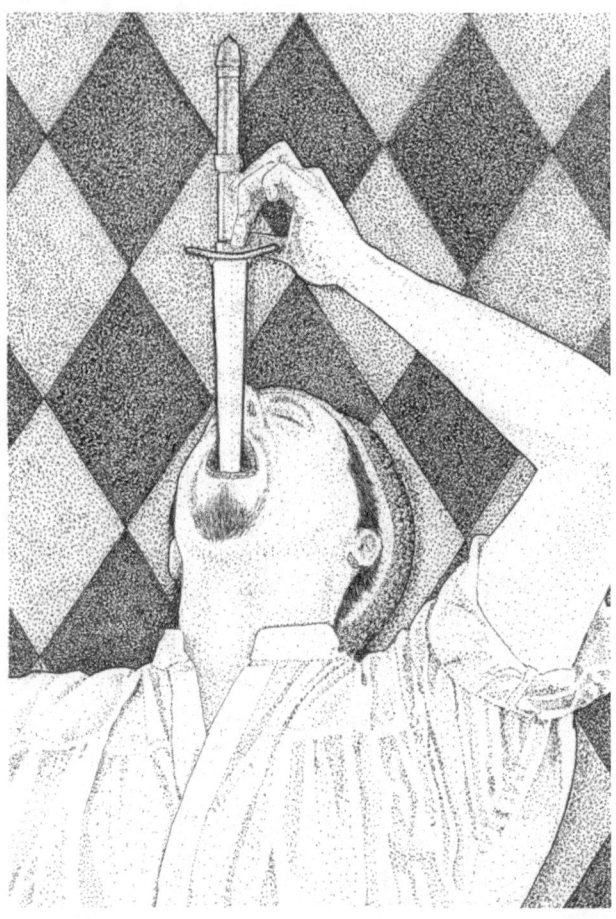

He held his out arms in the shape of the cross. I heard the gravel grind beneath me as I shuffled my feet. The jester then re-moved the sword, re-sheathed it, and said, "Those who live by the sword will die by the sword, but those who swallow their sword are liable to get a sword throat!"

For failures and fools.

Epilogue: Mistake

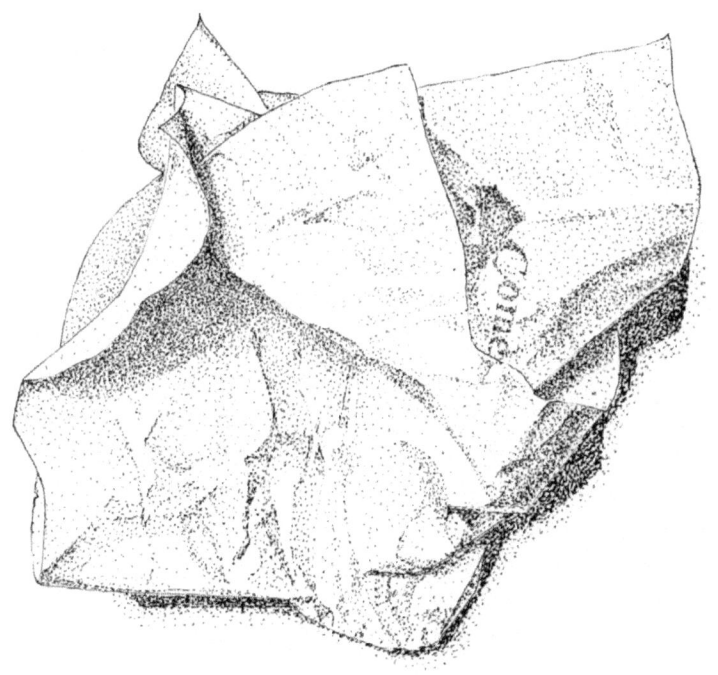